THE ARK

by the same author

THE ARK

THE SHOOTING STAR

ROWAN FARM

THE WICKED ENCHANTMENT

CASTLE ON THE BORDER

BLUE MYSTERY

THE LONG WAY HOME

DANGEROUS SPRING

A TIME TO LOVE

MARGOT BENARY-ISBERT

The Ark

TRANSLATED BY CLARA AND RICHARD WINSTON

GLOUCESTER, MASS.

PETER SMITH

1987

CONTENTS

THE ARK

CHAPTER ONE

The House in Parsley Street

THE WIND swept around the corners and chased clouds of dust out of the ruins of bombed houses. The cold, clinging darkness of the October evening dropped down upon the strange city from a leaden sky. The streets were deserted. Nobody was out who could possibly help it.

Nevertheless, the little band of people who were walking toward the center of the town was in high spirits. The two girls, Margret and Andrea, walked ahead, chatting gaily with one another. Behind them came their small, dark-haired mother, holding Joey's hand and trying to answer his endless questions. "Will we have a stove, too, Mummy? Will there be other kids there to play with? And if I have to begin school, can I just stay out if I don't like it?"

"You'll like it well enough," his mother said. "It's about time a big boy like you learned to read and write, now you're going on seven. You want to, don't you?"

"I'm not sure," Joey said dubiously. "After all, Tom

Thumb never went to school, and he was smarter than the man-eater."

Margret, who was holding the slip of paper from the Housing Office, crossed the street and the others followed her. " 'Down the street by the station,' the man said, 'as far as the square with the trees.' You see, there are the trees. 'Then the first street to the right and the second to the left.' "

"Parsley Street Number 13," Andrea cried, dancing a little jig, as though the address alone contained wonderful and mysterious possibilities.

"Parsley Street sounds nice, doesn't it, Joey," Mother said.

"It sounds green and good to eat. Tell me a story about it."

"Wait a while, we'll be there soon."

Since noon they had stood around in the big, cold gymnasium where the refugees were being assigned quarters. The mothers with little babies had to be taken care of first, of course. But finally their turn had come. After nine months of moving from place to place, from refugee camp to refugee camp, they would now be getting something that could be called a home. Not their own apartment, of course; the cities of West Germany were so crowded that they could not hope for anything like that. But at least they would have their own room. In fact two! Two rooms all to themselves—it was almost too good to be true. Rooms without a crowd of other people, of squabbling women and crying children. How wonderful it will be to be by ourselves, Margret thought, sighing to herself. What would Parsley Street and the house itself be like? The various barracks where they had stayed had always been full of such bad smells. There had been only a small space for each family, and people had to keep potatoes and their supply of firewood under the cots, and hang what few clothes they had on a string above the tattered straw mattress.

"Where are we going now?" the children had asked each time they and their belongings were loaded into a cattle car. No one had known. "Somewhere," had always been the answer.

At home, in Father's book case, there had been a book about the wanderings of Ulysses. Ulysses, too, had wandered about the world for many years after a war before he finally found his way back home. The *Odyssey* had been one of Margret's favorite books. She used to read it over and over with her brother Christian, and they had acted out the parts. Then they had wanted to have wonderful adventures like Ulysses. But now Margret herself had become almost a Ulysses, traveling homeless through the world, and it was not nearly so marvelous as she had imagined. "In fact it has been horrible," she said with a shudder, speaking more to herself than to her sister Andrea who trudged cheerfully along at her side— a slender little girl with her mother's dark hair and her father's blue eyes. She wasn't ten yet—ages younger than Margret, who would soon be all of fourteen.

"Why do you call it horrible?" Andrea asked. "It's been lots of fun—going to so many different places and having so many train rides and so many other children to play with. Joey has always loved it."

Margret nodded. Of course, the younger children had enjoyed it. They hardly remembered what a decent, orderly life was like. They didn't even notice how terribly thin Mother had become, or how much grey there was in her hair. What would Father say about the way Mummy looked when he came back from Russia? "Take good care of your Mummy for me," he had told the three older children when he had had to leave them. That was three years ago now. Margret's thoughts kept returning to this, and she gave her mother a look of deep concern. "You've gotten so terribly thin," she said. "There's hardly anything left of you."

"There's still plenty of me here, don't worry," Mother said, and for a moment little sparks of gold danced in her eyes— the way they used to whenever Father teased her. "I can keep going for quite a while yet, my big girl. I have to, until you learn to sew on the buttons for your brother and sister. Look, there's another one coming off Joey's jacket."

Margret's forehead wrinkled in a frown. "I'd just like to know one time when something isn't coming off Joey," she said. Being a big sister was just about the worst thing that could happen to a person. As if it weren't hard enough already being a girl. Nobody asked Matthias to sew on buttons. On the other hand, of course, he had to split wood and pull the little cart which held the family's baggage—and sometimes even Joey on top of the baggage.

"See if you can read that street sign across the street, Margret," Mother said. "There's just enough light from that window. It can't be much further."

"If it is much further I'm going to cry," Joey threatened. "I'm hungry and I'm cold."

"Cry!" Andrea exclaimed. "What a baby!"

"This is Capuchin Street," Margret called from across the way. "The man at the gym said it's one block after Capuchin Street."

"Look at the slip again."

"Number Thirteen Parsley Street. Mrs. Verduz, the widow

of Chief Municipal Secretary Verduz. He must have been something very important, Mother."

"Now you must make a good impression, children," Mother said, and she examined her flock with a worried expression. Her family looked rather wild and ill-kempt, and the wildest looking of them all, big Matthias, was not here yet. It was impossible to take care of clothes that were being worn all the time. During their brief stay with relatives in Hamburg there had been a chance for all of them to rest up and get clean—but all traces of that visit had long since vanished. Hamburg had been full of occupation troops and it had been impossible to get a permit to stay there. Mother had worn out the precious soles of her shoes going from one official to the next, but in vain. They had been assigned to Hesse and to Hesse they had to go; there was no help for it.

Mother sighed. "It's a good thing Matthias won't be coming with the cart for a while," she said reflectively. "I'm glad I won't have to introduce our whole horde at once to the poor landlady. We'll go down better a spoonful at a time. I feel sorry for her already."

"I don't," Andrea said firmly. "She ought to be glad. We're a very nice family, I think."

"I wish you wouldn't tell her so right off, Andrea," Mother said. "Perhaps she'll notice it herself."

And then they were in it—Parsley Street, a little lane like something out of a picture book. Almost all the houses were undamaged. They were pressed right up against one another as if they had given each other support through the perils of war. Most of them were half-timber houses, with wide flat surfaces of mortar between the dark old beams. In the yellow lamplight from the many windows the family saw that a large number of the beams were carved or painted in bright colors. Beneath the steep gables the attic windows looked out like peering eyes. The doors were painted brown or green, and the hardware on them was shiny brass.

"It must be that one," Margret said. "The skinny little one that looks sort of crooked. Yes, see, there it is: Number Thirteen."

The little house really looked as if it were hunchbacked. It leaned its left shoulder against the house next to it as though it were tottering and feeble from old age. On the great beam that supported the first floor was painted the date 1683, and in intricate lettering was a motto which could not be read in the dim light.

"An historical house," Andrea exclaimed, her eyes sparkling. "Just think of how many things must have happened in it in almost three hundred years. Maybe even a murder," she added hopefully. "Probably there's a ghost. I'd like to see a real ghost."

"I don't like ghosts," Joey said perversely.

"Anyway, Andrea will find out about everything that has ever happened in the house before we've been here three days," Margret said knowingly.

"Let me ring," Joey cried when he saw the gleaming brass bell pull. He pulled it. Inside a little bell tinkled. Then for a while nothing happened. What if nobody were home and they had to stand out in the street and wait? Joey was so over-tired he would certainly start to cry. Even the older girls were shivering with cold, and all of them were hungry. The icy wind seemed to reach through their clothes right into their bones.

"Ring again, Joey," Mother said.

Maybe it's an enchanted house and you have to do everything three times, Margret thought. Three was her number, her own secret, magic number; it banished the bad and brought all good things. She had three stars of her own, the stars of Orion's belt. Those stars had stood above the Polish camp where her mother had had to work when she was separated from the children. Matthias had been sent elsewhere, to a men's camp, and for a long time they did not know what was happening to him. Joey and the two girls had been sent to live with a peasant family near the Polish camp. There the girls had had to work hard, but otherwise conditions were pretty decent. And on winter nights the three stars had shone down upon Margret steadfastly. After three months Mother had finally come back to them. Not all those in the camp returned. Many had been buried on the heath. Mother's face was grey and her hair had turned grey, and the gloss had gone out of it. But she was alive, she was back with them, and as if by a miracle Matthias, too, found his way back to them—because the good stars had watched over them.

But where had the stars been before that on the May night when Margret's twin brother Christian was shot, and with him their Great Dane who had leaped at the first of the men who came rushing into the house? Those two, Christian and the dog, Cosi, had been closer to Margret than anyone else, her companions from babyhood. And now she was alone. She never mentioned their names, never spoke of the days when all of them had been together.

"Three times!" she thought, and she rang the bell again.

Immediately they heard a door creaking and footsteps

coming downstairs. Margret's heart pounded. If only Mrs. Verduz would be friendly. "Be nice," she murmured as if she were saying a spell. "Please be nice, be nice."

"What's that, Margret?" her mother asked.

"Nothing. You see, someone is opening the door."

The door opened just a tiny crack, hardly big enough for a mouse to slip through. "What do you want?" asked a voice which was just as thin as the crack of the door.

"Good evening," Mother said.

"Good evening," the children's three voices echoed.

"We were sent here, we're to live in your house," Mother explained.

The door opened a few inches more. A tall thin woman stuck her head out and stared at the group. "Is that so?" she said. "You are to live here? Is it possible?"

The light from the hallway fell upon her thin figure. She was wearing a grey dress with a ruche of black lace down the front. She seemed to have stepped right out of great-grandmother's photograph album. An odd-looking pair of glasses hung from a silk ribbon pinned to her dress. These glasses, their mother later explained, were called pince-nez, meaning pinch-the-nose. The lady set them on her nose so that she could see better.

"Good Heavens!" she exclaimed. "Four persons! What are those people at the Housing Office thinking of. I was promised a childless couple. It must be an error."

"No, here it is written down," Margret said, showing her slip of paper. "Here, you see, is the name: Mrs. Verduz. You are Mrs. Verduz, aren't you? And the rooms have been under requisition for a long time."

"No, no, no," the lady cried, raising her hands imploringly.

"This is impossible. Four persons! Why, I have only two beds."

"Five persons," Mother said. The grey old lady might as well be told all the dreadful truth at once. "My oldest boy is coming along later on. I'm very sorry we have to invade you at night this way, but there's nothing to be done about it now. The children have been standing around all day; they're tired and frozen, and where else could we go for the night? There's no one left in the gymnasium by this time, and the barracks are already filled up with new people."

"Well, since that's how things stand I suppose you can come in for the night," Mrs. Verduz said unwillingly. "Tomorrow I shall have to go down to the Housing Office right away and explain the mistake."

They climbed the steep staircase. Along the walls hung pictures and devout mottoes in handsome carved frames. On the landing stood two large tubs in which green plants were growing. A big black cat slipped silently between them.

"What a beautiful cat," Margret cried softly. "Andrea, look at the wonderful cat."

She crouched down on a step and coaxed the cat to come to her. Its amber eyes blinked at her; then, with head stretched forward, it cautiously approached and graciously permitted Margret to scratch it behind the ears.

"That's Caliph," the lady said without turning. "He never lets strangers touch him."

"All animals let Margret touch them," Andrea said. Mrs. Verduz turned her head and her eyebrows shot up, half in surprise, half in pleasure. For a moment she looked quite human.

On the ground floor there were two doors, on the second

floor three. The third floor was the attic, and here also there were three doors. Mrs. Verduz opened the one opposite the stairs and silently pointed to a spacious room filled with an odd assortment of furniture. It had two windows overlooking Parsley Street, and Andrea rushed over to look out. There was real glass in them, and each had a pair of faded curtains. In one corner stood a drum stove. In the brass lamp, which had once been a kerosene lamp, there was actually an electric bulb! Mrs. Verduz switched on this lamp as they entered. On both sides of the room the wall sloped sharply down, following the line of the roof.

"How lovely," Andrea said impulsively. Margret glanced reprovingly at her. But what was wrong with saying that the room was attractive, with its big, grey-and-red figured sofa, carved chairs and other old-fashioned things?

Mrs. Verduz raised her glasses to her nose again and studied Andrea with a pleased air. "The bedroom adjoins," she said in an almost kindly tone. "Yes, it is a very fine apartment, but there are only two beds; it won't do for five persons."

The bedroom was narrow. Two beds stood against the long wall, and beneath the small window was a stand which held an enamel washbasin. In one corner were a small table and two chairs.

"We could put one of the beds in the living room," Mother said—and Margret realized that Mother hoped to be able to stay here. "The sofa can be moved in here for Matthias, one bed for the two girls, and the other in the big room for Joey and me. That would do it."

"But I want to sleep with Matthias," Joey said.

"You can later, but this winter I want you sleeping in the

warm room so that you won't get any more sore throats."

Downstairs the bell rang. "That's Matthias," Andrea cried, and went clattering down the steps. She could have done it less noisily, because the banisters were perfect for sliding down without a sound. But Andrea had not quite dared to slide because Mother had said they must make a good impression.

"Quiet, Andrea!" Margret called after her—but the warning was already too late. Andrea did not see Mrs. Verduz's face or she would have realized why her sister had called out.

"I'm so sensitive about noise after all the bombings," Mrs. Verduz said. "That is one reason I cannot endure children in the house. I suppose you have your linen with you, Mrs. . . . what was your name again?"

"Lechow," Mother said. "No, no linen, unfortunately . . ."

Mrs. Verduz shook her head in silent disapproval. Not only was her house being filled up with strangers to whom she had to entrust all this good furniture, but on top of it all she would have to let them use her bed linen too.

"We have one wool blanket each," Margret said hastily. "We can get along without sheets. We did in camp."

"Sleep without sheets!" Mrs. Verduz said with a frown. "Not in my house. What would happen to my good mattresses?" With a sigh she went across to the spare attic room. She could be heard rattling keys. Margret winked at her mother and whispered, "Sheets, Mummy! And featherbeds, too—see them all folded up? We won't leave here, no matter how disagreeable she is. And besides the cat is so nice." She bent down and stroked Caliph, who purred and rubbed against her ankles. Obviously it was a case of mutual love at first sight.

Mrs. Verduz returned with a bundle of linen in her arms
—snowy white sheets and bright-colored coverlets. The linen
smelled rather musty, as though it had not been used for
many years.

Matthias was coming up the stairs with Andrea. Between
the two of them they were carrying one of the two sacks
which contained the family's precious possessions—the wool
blankets, some underwear and the one spare set of clothing
each owned. Their bread and the rest of their provisions
were distributed among their rucksacks. Now they would be
getting regular food ration cards, just like the people who
belonged here.

Matthias had tucked his precious violin case under his arm
and parked the cart in the small courtyard back of the house.
Matthias always got the hang of places quickly.

"This is my oldest boy, Matthias," Mother said, and Matthias removed the cap from his blond shock of hair and
made a bit of a bow. Margret felt proud of him. Not that she
personally placed much importance on fine manners. But if
the grey lady didn't let them stay—no, she couldn't bear to
think of that! Manners were a small price to pay, if only they
could stay.

"Oh, the dirt all these children will track in," Mrs. Verduz
wailed, and her face twisted up as though she had a tooth-
ache.

"We can always take our shoes off downstairs," Margret
suggested.

"And I can sweep the stairs on Saturdays," Andrea said.
"I won't mind that a bit."

"Yes," Mrs. Verduz said. "I really cannot be expected
to clean up after other people. My maid has just up and

left me again. There's no depending on people any more."

"The girls will be glad to help with the work," Mother said.

"That would be fine," Mrs. Verduz replied. The prospect evidently pleased her. (She'll keep us, she'll keep us, Margret rejoiced.) "Yes, I certainly could use a little help in the house. And perhaps the big boy could split some wood now and then and bring it in."

Margret gave Matthias a suggestive poke with her elbow. "I'll do that," he said, nodding. "And me too," Joey promised. "I can split wood and carry it in too—I'm almost seven."

"Well, then, you may as well get settled for the night," the grey lady said, with gracious condescension. "We'll see what tomorrow brings. Good night. Come, Caliph!"

As soon as she had gone Andrea took a hop, skip and jump. "It's fine here, I like it," she exclaimed happily, and dropped down on the sofa to test the springs.

"Be careful of the furniture," Mother warned her. "What do you say, Margret?"

"She's a witch," Margret said darkly.

Mother shook her head. "Just imagine what *we* would have said if an utter stranger with four wild-looking children were suddenly quartered on us and we had to give them our own bed linen besides."

"Why, Mummy!" both girls exclaimed together, and Margret added, "You would probably have said, 'How nice of you to drop in.' And you would at least have offered a good hot drink to people as frozen as we are."

Silently, Matthias unpacked their provisions. He could never see why other people talked so much.

"Eat quickly, children," Mother said. "I'm looking forward so much to sleeping in a real bed again that I can hardly wait. Do you girls still remember how to make a bed?"

"We'll learn again," Andrea said. "I used to do the crib for the Polish woman. But the big beds were never made up as long as we were there, and we slept in the hay, thank Heaven."

"Tomorrow I'll go to the Economic Office about wood and potatoes," Matthias said. "When we have something to run the stove with, it will be nice and comfortable here."

Margret was sure it would be comfortable. Mother would have made a tent in the desert pleasant to live in.

"Then can we stay here?" Joey asked. "And will Father be able to find us?"

"Of course he'll find us," Mother assured him. "We left a trail of pebbles behind us, like Hansel and Gretel."

"Oh, tell me the story, Mummy." While listening, Joey chewed away at a thick slice of bread spread with fake liverwurst.

"You know that we wrote our names down everywhere, wherever we passed. In the camps and in the homes of the relatives in Berlin and Hamburg. And we left our names at the Red Cross and at the railroad stations. All Father has to do is to track us down. And now we'll write letters to all those places again and give our new address, 13 Parsley Street. But go get some water now, children, so we can wash up. I saw the faucet right outside in the hall, to the left of the stairs."

"Wash up?" Andrea and Joey said slowly, and Joey suddenly remembered that he was terribly tired.

"It's really too cold here to wash," Margret said.

Matthias, who was to sleep on the sofa, had already undressed and slipped under the blanket. "Good night," he said.

The others went to the bedroom, and while Mother helped a sleepy Joey to undress, the two girls skillfully made the beds.

"Do you think she'll keep us?" Margret asked as she slipped under the featherbed. "Don't you think she has to? There's nothing she can do about an order from the Housing Office."

"Everything will turn out all right," Mother said. "Isn't it good to be lying in a bed again?"

Andrea pressed close against Margret. The bedding was uncomfortably clammy, but gradually she began to feel warmer. "Being a refugee is very nice after all," she murmured, her teeth chattering.

"Nice?" Margret asked.

"Yes, you know there's something new every day. I've always wanted to live in an old house like this. And at home we were never allowed to sleep together and I'd freeze to death if I had to sleep alone tonight."

"Joey is asleep already," Mother called out. "Good night. We have a lot to do tomorrow." She shifted about once or twice, as though savoring the pleasure of stretching out in a real bed. Then there was no further sound. Andrea, too, fell asleep instantly. Like a warm little animal, she snuggled up to her sister, breathing softly. Margret alone remained awake, conscious of the calm, healthy, warm little body of her sister. What a happy creature Andrea was, carrying her house on her back like a snail, feeling at home wherever she was. I will never feel at home anywhere again, Margret thought.

Home—that meant the old orchard under the expanse of clear sky in Pomerania, the white house on the outskirts of the town, Father's roses on the edge of the terrace where the family took their breakfast on warm summer days. Cosi would lie in the sun and drink in its warmth. And there was Christian, too. But all this, this strange city with its ruined streets, this old, old house with its steep stairway, this grey old woman who disliked their coming—this could never be home, could it?

Outside came the cries of the owls—many of them had nested in the ruins. Hoo, hoohoohoo, they cried, and it seemed to Margret that the city itself was wailing a complaint against the grey army of refugees who had descended upon it, and who had to be found room for. Suddenly Margret felt afraid. She was tempted to call to her mother as she used to when she was a small child, whenever something frightened her. But no, of course it would not do to wake Mother up. Mother was so tired, and Margret would not even have been able to say what she was afraid of. She listened to the silence of the sleeping house. Outside something rattled. A floorboard creaked. From the times she had spent in her grandparents' farmhouse in Silesia Margret knew that old houses often began to speak at night. Perhaps Caliph the cat was stalking about. What a beautiful animal he was, and how friendly he had been to her right away. Perhaps things were really not so bad. What was it the grey lady had said? He doesn't let strangers touch him! Margret smiled at this, and smiling, she fell asleep.

CHAPTER TWO

The Chronicles of Parsley Street

FOR SOME TIME the children did not know whether Mrs.
Verduz intended to let them stay. Probably Mother herself
did not know. Margret and Matthias gave the grey lady a
wide berth and tried their best not to attract attention. But
Andrea and Joey felt curiously drawn to her, and did not
seem to notice that their landlady had no love for children.
To Joey she seemed a fabulous monster, dangerous and
powerful. It would not have surprised him if her grey figure
had suddenly dissolved into thin air, or if she had changed
herself into a small grey mouse. Spellbound, he crept about
after her. What did she keep in the mysterious locked room
on the ground floor? What was she cooking in the pot in her
kitchen which sent forth such alluring smells? What marvelous things was she digging up out of the boxes and cupboards in the crowded attic spare room?

Alas, she had to do a good deal of rummaging in the attic,
for the Lechows were always asking for something. They
had no pots and no plates, no spoons or forks or cups or

brooms. Mother was constantly sending Andrea to Mrs. Verduz to ask the landlady to lend them something. The children knew that Mrs. Verduz did not lend things gladly. But what else could they do but borrow? It was impossible to get any priority certificates at the Economic Office. Margret had tried; during their first few days in Parsley Street she had stood in line for hours, but without the slightest success. There just were no supplies.

Andrea liked to go borrowing, because something interesting always happened. It was an adventure to trail the grey old lady into the hidden corners of the old house where generations had left behind fascinating fragments of their lives. What an accumulation of things, all in good order and freshly mothproofed every spring, there was in that attic room. There was even a bookcase jammed with the yellowed schoolbooks of children who were now distant ancestors, and the books that had belonged to Mrs. Verduz's husband were here also. Andrea would look greedily at them whenever she saw them. And there were chests filled with Mr. Verduz's suits and the widow's own discarded clothes. "You don't easily part with such things," Mrs. Verduz would say. "There are too many memories clinging to them." And Andrea fancied she could see the memories actually clinging to all those old things. Perhaps the dusty and faintly moldy smell was the odor of memories.

Whenever Andrea brought something back with her, she would say to Mother, "Be careful of these things; there are memories clinging to them."

Every time she gave something away, Mrs. Verduz sighed heavily, and Andrea sighed with her out of sympathy, and looked up at her with tilted head, her blue eyes beneath the smooth black hair full of timid appeal. Andrea could put on such a sweet look that people quite forgot she was anything but an angel—that in fact she was a wild little creature with a head full of notions, gangling arms and legs which grew so fast that Mother was continually letting down the hems of her dresses.

Sometimes Andrea allowed Joey to come with her. She would hold his hand tightly while she made her request to Mrs. Verduz and while the landlady mournfully rummaged through her treasures. Sometimes Andrea had to pinch Joey to keep him quiet, for Joey had the inquisitiveness of all the Lechow children.

"What do you have in the big box?" Joey asked once.

"The suits of my husband, who is now in Heaven."

"If we had a whole box full of suits we would be in Heaven, too," Joey said wisely. "And what does the motto on the beam of the house say?"

"Welcome to all who are happy here!"

"We're happy here," Joey said. "A nice motto— Ouch, Andrea, why are you pinching me so hard?"

"Things were different in those days," Mrs. Verduz said, bending over a chest full of kitchen utensils. With many warnings to treat the loans with care, the children were dismissed and returned in triumph to their mother. "There's still a lot left," Andrea said coolly. "You can send me again soon."

They were certainly lucky to have come to a house where there were so many useful things to be borrowed, though Mrs. Verduz was not one of those people the Bible speaks of, one of the cheerful givers whom God loves. But she gave, even if not cheerfully, and probably half of Andrea's pleasure in her dealings with the grey landlady came from the atmosphere of suspense and uncertainty that surrounded each of these encounters.

"We just have to ask her straight out whether she's going to keep us," Andrea said one day. She was quite ready to put the question herself.

Margret was alarmed. "What are you thinking of, Miss Freshy," she said. "We've got to be good and careful not to remind her that she wanted a childless couple. Maybe that will slip her mind. All we can do is be terribly nice and help her all we can."

This the children did, each in his own fashion. Andrea almost floated up the stairs, and going down she used the banister as often as possible. She was as noiseless as an elf, she thought—and she made sure everyone noticed. Andrea enjoyed making believe she was an elf, but that was not her only part. When she swept the stairs, as she had promised to do, she was nothing less than an enchanted princess who had to work as maidservant for a wicked witch. It was sometimes hard for the rest of the family to know what Andrea was at any given time. She could ask in so sharp a voice, "But can't you see I'm a princess?" that everyone felt quite foolish for not having realized it at once.

The first job Matthias had was to build a little shelf by the cellar stairs. This was where the Lechow children were to place their shoes when they entered the house, so that they would not make noise or track in dirt.

Before the first week was over, Margret was doing all the shopping for Mrs. Verduz. "You don't mind, do you, since you're going out anyhow?" Mrs. Verduz asked. "Standing in line is so hard for me, with my rheumatism."

Often her plaintive voice could be heard calling through the house, "Matthias, would you mind splitting a little more wood today?" Or, "Andrea, the stairs are all dirty again. That's because of all the people in the house." Or, "Margret, would you mind running over to the bakery for me, and the vestibule needs cleaning again."

And finally, "My dear Mrs. Lechow, Andrea has told me you're very good at sewing. I haven't a thing to wear any more, and seamstresses will work only for people who bring them butter and bacon."

Mother was grateful for the chance to repay her landlady for all the loans. "I'd be glad to sew for you, Mrs. Verduz, if only I had a sewing machine," she said.

That was a difficulty easily remedied. Mrs. Verduz offered to lend her sewing machine to Mother; it took up too much space in the parlor anyhow. "I'll bring something up to you tomorrow," Mrs. Verduz said. "We can deduct the work from the rent."

Then she sat down in the kitchen over a cup of real coffee —she had a distant relation in America who occasionally sent her a package. She sat with Caliph on her lap while Andrea did the dishes, and she sighed heavily. "It's so hard having so many strangers in the house. If my husband knew . . ."

"He must know," Andrea said. "People in Heaven know everything."

"I suppose your papa is in Heaven too?"

"Oh no, he's in Russia. He'll be coming back soon. Then, you'll see, he'll take care of your headaches, because he's a doctor."

Mrs. Verduz suffered from frequent headaches because of all the people in the house.

"Have you had news that he's still alive?"

"Well, not directly. The mail in Russia isn't like it is here. Everything is so far away—as far away as . . ." Andrea tried to think of a comparison . . . "as your relation who sends you coffee. That's why we don't hear from the prisoners. But he'll surely be coming soon."

"Do you think so?" Mrs. Verduz asked.

Andrea was certain.

The coffee filled the room with its fragrance. Caliph purred. Andrea went on rattling the dishes. Now that Mrs. Verduz knew that Andrea was the child of a doctor, she began talking about her husband's last illness, his operation and his death, and Andrea asked sensible and sympathetic questions. She was the most attentive listener in the world, and since the subject was endlessly interesting to Mrs. Verduz, the grey old lady gradually developed something that was almost a liking for Andrea.

While they were talking, Matthias and Joey came in with a heavy basket full of split wood. They worked silently, like two men. For Joey it was sheer glory to be able to help his big brother whom he worshipped and imitated. It was his job to pack the split wood into the basket and later to pile it up by the kitchen stove. As far as he was concerned, it would have been wonderful if life could go on this way forever. But in their second week on Parsley Street fate caught up with him. Without even talking the thing over, his mother took him by the hand one day and registered him at school. Time and again he had complained over the way his sisters were always pestering him with writing and arithmetic whenever they had a quiet minute. They just loved to make him miserable, he had protested, and had done his best to get out of learning anything. But now he was glad to have had at least an introduction to these difficult subjects, since he was so far behind the rest of his class.

Andrea was one of a group of girls who were given an examination by the school board. She came home radiant and told her mother the board had decided she was ready for the lycée.

"What are you talking about?" Margret said. "You know we have no money for the lycée."

Andrea nodded, suddenly subdued, and Mother looked very sad. But three days later there came a letter from the school board requesting Miss Andrea Lechow to report to the High School of the Ursuline nuns, which was offering a scholarship for a refugee child. There she was given another examination by the Abbess and the teacher of her class. When she came home, she said, "They were just delighted with me and they're taking me."

Mother stroked her black hair and said, "You've been lucky again, Andrea. Now you must really work hard."

Nobody knew what was going to become of Margret, least of all Margret herself. In the old days she had wanted to go on with school and study to be a veterinarian. She loved animals, especially sick and weak ones. All her life she had been bringing home starving cats and birds that had fallen out of the nest, and nursing them along. Even when she was a little girl, neighborhood people had brought injured animals to her.

But now two years had passed since she had had any proper schooling. By the winter of 1944 things had been

tense in East Germany, in Pomerania, and in the early
months of 1945, when the Russians came closer, the great
exodus had begun. Most of their friends had got out as fast
as they could, but Mother had been among the few who
stayed. It had been wintertime and terribly cold, and she
had been afraid to expose the children to the dangers of
flight. Instead of running away, she had stayed and worked
for the Polish doctor who took over their house and Father's
practice. But after a few months she had been sent to a camp
anyway.

Now Margret would soon be fourteen, and nobody quite
knew whether she ought to go back to grammar school until
the end of the current school year, or whether she would be
exempted altogether. But if she were exempted, what would
she do then? Her mother asked her whether she wanted to
learn to sew. Mother herself was clever at sewing, although
she had never had any instruction in it. Already people were
coming from all over the neighborhood and bringing her
clothes to repair and remake. Mrs. Verduz's own wardrobe
had quickly been brought up to par, and now Mrs. Verduz's
only complaint was that the rest of Mrs. Lechow's clientele
were almost all refugee women whom she had met in camp
—and who could not pay.

If Margret would learn dressmaking, Mother thought,
they would certainly be able to pull the family through all
hard times until Father came home. But Margret looked so
unhappy when she thought of sitting at a sewing machine
day after day that Mother decided to put off making any
decision.

In any case, there was plenty for Margret to do. It was
really lucky that she was free and could help around the

house. She shared with Matthias the wearisome job of waiting in line for rations and of going to the various ration boards. She did all the errands and shopping; she also cooked their simple meals so that Mother could work longer at her sewing. The stairs had to be swept, the hall scrubbed, Mrs. Verduz's kitchen cleaned and her dishes washed, and Andrea had little time for these things now that she was going to school. In fact, there was almost more work than Margret could manage. But in return Mrs. Verduz gave her lunch twice a week, and then her hungry brothers and sisters could eat her ration.

One of her great consolations in all this work was Caliph, who constantly kept her company. Purring, he rubbed around her legs when she swept the stairs, or sat on the topmost step looking at her and talking to her in friendly meows whenever she bent down to stroke his satiny head. They got on beautifully together, and Mrs. Verduz said, "I don't know what has gotten into him; he keeps running after you all day long."

Nothing had been decided about Matthias' future either. At one time he had wanted to be an aviator—in fact a parachute jumper. But since the time his father had taken him to Berlin—he was ten then—and shown him the planetarium, his sole ambition was to become an astronomer. He even worked hard at mathematics because his father had told him that anyone who hoped to study astronomy had to know mathematics. Every night at home, when the sky was clear, he had sat on the old wall in the garden and watched the movements of the mysterious worlds above. His father had told him the names of many of the stars, and on his birthday presented him with a map of the heavens which he

still had with him. He had read everything he could find
about the stars, and when his school got hold of a telescope
he had spent night after night with the science teacher on
the roof of the school, making observations.

But now there was no use thinking about their former
plans. Matthias knew as well as Margret that they were poor,
even poorer than the Polish farmers at home whom Father
used to treat free of charge.

"If I can't study astronomy, the next best thing would be
to become a gardener," Matthias told Mother. He had always liked working with their old Polish gardener and helping his father graft roses.

He had gone to the Labor Office and called on almost all
the nurseries in town, but there was no job open for an
apprentice. The officials at the Labor Office told him he
ought to learn to be a mason; construction workers were
most in demand now. But Mother had managed to put that
off, too; during their first weeks Matthias was needed at
home.

Without Matthias, there really would have been nobody
to fetch wood and potatoes for the family. He was out with
their little cart all day. But it was the end of October; the
dealers in town already had all the orders they could fill and
none of them wanted to take on a new customer, especially
a stranger. The only thing for the Lechows to do was to go
to the farmers on the outskirts of the town. After making
many inquiries, Margret and Matthias wheeled their cart
through town and out into the countryside one day, toward
the hills that reared up like a gigantic wave against the clear
autumnal sky. It was a good two-hour walk to the village of
Hellborn, but the children enjoyed getting out of the grey

ruined streets of the city and breathing the fresh country air.

The woods on the slopes of the mountains were glowing with autumnal color. The rowans which lined the country roads were heavy with coral clumps of berries; the air was crystal clear, and above the harvested fields hung blue-grey clouds of smoke from burning potato vines.

"This is just how it would smell at home at this time of year," Matthias said.

Margret nodded. "Yes, and just like Grandma and Grandpa's house in Silesia the times we used to go there for our fall vacation and help with the potato harvest. Do you think they are still living?"

"If they were, we would have heard from them long ago," Matthias said.

They fell silent and their thoughts went back to the wonderful holidays they used to spend with their mother's parents. Their grandfather had kept two ponies for his grandchildren, and the most wonderful part of those wonderful vacations had been riding over the fields early in the morning with Cosi and Grandfather's hunting dogs scampering round the horses.

They had been told that the blacksmith at Hellborn might be willing to part with some of his potatoes. But when they arrived, the smith had gone out to plow and his young wife did not know whether there were any potatoes left for sale, or whether all had been already promised. Margret said a quick, earnest prayer to herself that there might be some left —for what in the world would they do if they could get no potatoes. You couldn't eat ration certificates. They sat down on the steps of the farmhouse and waited. Wherever you went you had to wait—that was something they had learned long ago. Half your life is spent in waiting, Margret thought.

The October sun shone warmly down upon them as they sat there on the steps. Hens cackled around the yard, and some fat ducks paddled contentedly in the muddy water of a small shellhole. On the lawn a sheep was staked out. A young woman in the garden was stooping down to cut a plump purple cabbage. It was all so lovely and still. Everything had its place and belonged together, the animals and the people and the land, the garden with its cabbages and beanpoles, to which a few withered husks still clung, the strong smell from the barn and the gentle mooing of a cow. "I would like to stay here," Margret thought.

Matthias took half a loaf of bread and a paper twist of salt from his rucksack and they began eating their lunch. From the house across the road a girl came out carrying a cake tin as large as a wagon wheel. The whole village smelled of fresh bread and cake. It was Friday, when the week's baking was done.

The farm children stood around the yard and looked at the strangers. They nudged each other with their elbows, giggled and made frank remarks about this meal of dry bread. Finally Matthias threw such a fierce look at the pig-tailed little girls that they ran off, screeching.

At last the farmer came home, leading his handsome roan horse. Margret would have loved to stroke the animal and feel the softness of a horse's nose in her palm once more. But she was a stranger here and did not dare.

"Could you sell us some potatoes?" Matthias asked. The farmer's gaze passed over the tall, thin children, and he nodded. "Where are you from?" he asked.

"From Pomerania."

"They grow good potatoes there, don't they? How much does your little cart take?"

"Two hundred pounds. And if we can get the rest from you, we'll come again."

The man loaded their cart with two hundredweight, and threw in a few beets and cabbage heads. "I have to go to town next week anyhow," he said. "I'll bring you the rest of the potatoes—it'll all go in one load."

They thanked him profusely; they were so happy and relieved that they kept shaking his horny blacksmith's hand. "All right, all right," he said good-naturedly. "It don't matter to me whether I sell my spuds at the market or deliver them to you, so long as I get my ration stamps."

Mother was overjoyed when they came home with their precious load. "Just for once we'll celebrate," she said, and promptly put so large a pot of potatoes on the stove that each of them had as much as he wanted to eat.

"But from now on they have to be weighed every day," Matthias said. "Otherwise they won't even last until Easter."

The children had long ago grown used to never being quite filled. Sometimes they would wake in the middle of the night with a hollow feeling in their stomachs; but there was a good cure for that. You just had to hold your pillow tight against the hollow place; then at least you could go back to sleep.

The grey old lady still stalked about the crooked old house like a tall and terrible queen, never saying a word about her decision in regard to the family. In fact she had not made any decision; she had simply resigned herself to her harsh fate. And she had begun to realize that really it was not quite so harsh.

"So you're living with old lady Verduz?" the bakery woman whispered to Margret one day. "Why, good Lord, I certainly pity you."

Margret did not answer. She thought of the Lebenows, an old couple who lived in a damp cellar, and of Mrs. Krikoleit with her four small children who did not even have space enough for a third bed in the room—even if they had had the extra bed. And Margret thought that she and her family were pretty much in luck.

CHAPTER THREE

New Roots

THE LABOR OFFICE finally ordered Matthias to become a mason. They couldn't understand that he didn't at all want to be one. At least he managed to avoid being listed as an apprentice, for then he would have been committed for three years and he was still hoping for a miracle of some kind. At fifteen and a half he was now a helper, the lowest position of all the construction workers, lower even than the two apprentices who were the sons of master masons. It was hard work, but Matthias stuck at it although he often hated it. He earned a few marks and he could learn a good deal if he kept his eyes open. And at least he was free in case something better came along.

Cleaning bricks, carrying and handing up bricks, stirring mortar, standing from morning to night in the grey plaster dust of the ruins—that was the way he now earned his daily bread. It was hard for a boy who would rather have been looking at the stars.

"At least I'm doing something real for reconstruction," he

consoled himself. But he knew that he could not go on for long in this indefinite fashion. Sooner or later he would be caught and have to go to a trade school or something of the sort.

The men on the job were a mixed bunch. There was a foreman and three journeymen, the two apprentices, and finally a few released prisoners of war who had to put in their four weeks of reconstruction work—that was a city ordinance.

The men smoked cigarettes when they had any; they stooped to pick up the butts that Americans threw away. Their talk centered around their slender rations and how to improve them. They were all hungry, and the only people who could buy on the Black Market were those who had Black Market earnings. "Honest work," the men said sarcastically . . . "It's all right if you want to starve."

One way open to them was to do Black Market labor. On Saturdays and Sundays they went out to the country to repair some farmer's damaged stable wall or help pave a yard. Such work brought in more than their whole week's labor in the city. They would be given a good meal, cigarettes and even a loaf of bread or a bag of potatoes to carry home, and sometimes a bottle of creamy milk to take back for their children or younger brothers and sisters.

All the grey misery of the times came out in the conversations among these men and boys. During rest periods they played cards or told stories that Matthias did not like to listen to. But there was one young man who was different from the others—Matthias spotted him right away. His name was Dieter; he had a fine, honest face and friendly eyes, and he wore glasses. Matthias thought he must be twenty or twenty-one. He too was untrained, but he was quick and skillful, and the others often asked him for advice. They all respected and liked him, although he was not especially intimate with anyone. If he did not approve of something he said so in a quiet, almost humorous but very marked fashion.

One day he sat down at noon on a pile of boards and took out his guitar. He began playing and singing softly to himself. Matthias sat close by and watched him. He longed to get to know Dieter better.

Dieter seemed to sense this. "Come over here," he called. "I won't bite. Do you know this?" And he played Schubert's *Heath Rose*.

Matthias nodded eagerly and hummed the tune softly. He could never resist music, although his voice did not sound very good when he sang these days.

"So your voice is changing!" Dieter laughed. "But you're musical. Do you play an instrument?"

"The fiddle," Matthias said.

"Did you want to be a musician?"

"Oh, no hope of that," Matthias said. "I wanted to study astronomy. What about you?"

"Music. It's in my bones; I've never thought of anything else. My father was a conductor and my mother a pianist."

"And now?"

"Now it's building walls for us, my friend. Evenings I play the piano and sing in a café. Rather dingy place. But I get a plate of soup and earn a few marks. Would you like to join me?"

"If you think I can play well enough," Matthias said, flushing with pleasure until the tips of his ears were red.

"Come around to my place this evening and we'll see."

After work it turned out that they were going the same way. Dieter lived near Parsley Street.

"Everything is pretty much of a mess these days," he said to Matthias as they walked along. "We have to eat the stew others have cooked for us. We won't get anything for nothing, but wait and see, we'll make our way."

They played together several times. Matthias was out of practice, but the music did not turn out as badly as he had expected. His tall friend knew how to encourage and correct him. And one evening Dieter took him along to the café and introduced him to the owner. "Just give him a trial," he urged. "The music sounds a lot better with a violin. And if the guests like it, you'll pay him five marks a night and a good bowl of soup. Agreed?"

"Agreed," the owner boomed. He was a good-natured man who did not worry about a few marks more or less. Music was good for his business; his customers liked to hear a few cheerful melodies while they drank their bitter ersatz coffee. Music was refreshing after the hard, weary monotony of the day. And besides, it enabled people to talk about certain shady matters without being heard at the adjoining tables. Music was just fine—and few other restaurants in the city were so well patronized.

Three times a week Matthias played the violin at the café. He came home well fed and brought his mother the money. But what he liked best about it was being with Dieter.

At a corner table in the smoke-filled café a group of boys sat almost every evening. They played cards or swapped stamps and possibly also worked out Black Market deals, like almost all the customers. None of the boys could be much over eighteen, but they smoked cigarettes and apparently had well-filled wallets. Sometimes girls sat with them.

"I've been wonderng about these kids for quite a while," Dieter said to Matthias one evening. "They look as if they haven't any home. What's going to become of them if they go on this way?"

"It's not really any of our business," Matthias said.

"You think so? I thought you were smarter than that. What happens to these kids matters to all of us, don't you see?"

At home, Matthias constantly referred to his friend. He was all "Dieter says this" or "Dieter thinks that." His sisters became curious. "Has he any parents?" they asked. "Where does he live? When are you going to bring him around?"

"He comes from Berlin," Matthias said slowly, as though he were putting the story together. "I don't really know about his parents. I think they were both killed during the last weeks of the war. He doesn't talk about them much. Usually he talks about books and the theater and music—mostly music. He writes music, too."

"Marvelous," Andrea said. "Where does he live?"

"Near here, on Monk Street."

"But everything is smashed there."

"Well, they've fitted up a cellar—he and Hans."

"Who is this Hans?"

"A friend of his. He drives a truck. I think it's his own, the only thing he saved before the Russians took his farm in Thuringia. But the two of them have slipped across the zone border twice and got back all sorts of things that belonged to them. Beds and books and music and several instruments and two suitcases that Dieter had left with a friend. Now they've got their basement all set up nice and comfortable. They even have a stove."

"I have a friend too," Joey announced.

Life at school was no longer as awful as it had been. Joey was making his way hit or miss. He was not exactly winning any laurels, but he himself was quite satisfied with his success. His seatmate, Hans Ulrich, wasn't a genius either, but they stuck together through thick and thin, and if they did not exactly get the best marks, they made out pretty well in the schoolyard. For instance, there was Hänschen Fellber, the son of a café proprietor, who—everybody whispered— could smoke cigarettes without getting sick. That was quite an achievement, but it didn't give him the right to call Joey and his friend Hans "refugee bums." When Joey heard that he had rolled up his sleeves while the class stood around in tense excitement. Hänschen did not seem to be as good at boxing as at smoking, for Joey just tapped him on the nose and it began bleeding and Hänschen started to bawl. Joey was a little embarrassed by this overwhelming victory. Amid a respectful silence, he and Hans Ulrich left the battlefield. Back in the classroom, Joey expected a good whipping. But Hänschen did not tell on him; he remembered in time what the young teacher had said: "I want you all to be nice to the refugees."

Hans Ulrich was far and away the best athlete in the class, and that mattered more than being a good reader. He and Joey were the bravest when it came to letting themselves down into a buried cellar and crawling into holes from which they had to be pulled out again by the legs. They could walk along the top of a high wall without getting dizzy—that meant more than being able to smoke. Fortunately for his mother's peace of mind, Joey did not say too much at home about these feats. On the other hand, he never tired of singing Hans Ulrich's praises. Joey's mother had been wanting to make Hans' acquaintance for some time, but that was not so easy. Hans Ulrich was a busy person who always had to be up and doing. He had to get wood and potatoes, or even coal from the freightyards, which was quite a business because they kept good watch there and if you were caught it was too bad. There wasn't even much time for playing in the ruined house right behind the school. When he talked about this ruin, Joey's enthusiasm knew no bounds. He did not notice that his brother and sisters were making faces at him, trying to shut him up.

"Stop scaring the wits out of everybody, squirt," Matthias growled. And Margret said, "He'll make Mummy die of nervousness, and then what will we say when Father comes home."

"If that sort of thing could kill me, I'd have been dead long ago," Mother said. "Remember when you were Joey's age, Matthias, and they pulled you half drowned out of the river? And you, Margret, who used to crawl into doghouses to pet every chained dog you saw? And have you forgotten the time the three of you broke through the ice while skating?"

"Happy memories!" Matthias said.

"But we tried not to worry you that time, Mummy," Margret said. "We hung our clothes up on the willows. It was nice and sunny and we kept running around until our things were dry."

"Dry is something of an exaggeration," Mother said. "No, none of you were exactly quiet children, but I don't suppose

I would have exchanged you for all the model children in the world."

"You see," Joey said.

But his big brother had already carried him over to the corner. "Get to bed, squirt, it's way past time. When we were your age we had to be in bed on the dot of eight. I'm going to bed myself; I have to get up at six."

By now everything had been arranged as Joey had long hoped; he was allowed to sleep with Matthias, and Mother, who stayed up late over her sewing, slept alone in the living room.

Andrea had also made a friend in school. This friendship seemed to disprove the old proverb that birds of a feather flock together. In her class there was a plump little butcher's daughter named Lenchen Sauer who was utterly unlike Andrea in every way. She did not have an ounce of imagination and was not particularly good at any kind of mental work. She listened with utter amazement to Andrea's fanciful tales; she was, in fact, the best listener any storyteller could desire. Ordinarily Lenchen was a sturdy and cheerful creature, but when it came to reciting a poem or writing a theme or doing a simple English exercise, she had a hard time of it. On the other hand her dimpled, skillful hands could do things with darning and knitting needles that simply amazed Andrea. When Lench knitted a stocking it came out as smooth and regular as if it had been done by machine, while Andrea turned out a grey, knotty, twisted lump of cloth which Mother Lioba, the sewing teacher, held up to the class as a horrible example. Andrea did not take this to heart; she knew she was better at other things, and after all, nobody could be perfect.

One day Lenchen turned up at the Parsley Street house with an embarrassed and troubled air. It was her English homework—she simply couldn't do it. Andrea readily helped her, and soon got into the habit of going home with Lenchen to help her friend with any hard assignments. In the pleasant little room back of the butcher shop the two girls had space and quiet in which to work. Lenchen was an only child, and her fond parents were eager to repay Andrea for her assistance. Mother had forbidden Andrea to accept anything from them, but after all, having a glass of milk and a sandwich when it was offered to you could not be considered "accepting anything."

In general Andrea enjoyed a great deal of respect in her class. Not for her scholastic achievements; though she was bright enough she generally stayed just about in the middle, and the other girls had no reason to be jealous of her. She had other talents which made her popular. For example, she could do a kind of ventriloquism almost without moving her lips and was ready to support anyone who needed a little help. What she was most admired for was her imitations. She could imitate every one of the good nuns right up to the Mother Superior herself. She could even do a take-off on the Reverend Chaplain. Her imitations were never malicious—in fact they were hardly even exaggerated. Yet she noticed people's every trait and peculiarity and could act them out so skillfully that the class writhed with laughter. Sometimes, too, she put on little plays during recesses. All her friends would be given parts. She made up the plays herself, sometimes out of life and sometimes out of history or stories. Things were never dull when Andrea was around.

Thus three of the four Lechow children had already put

down new roots. Margret alone still had no friends her own age. She had never formed friendships easily, for she had always had her twin brother as a playmate. From their earliest days they had been inseparable, so much so that Margret had almost lost the ability to make friends. Christian and Cosi—how far away they were. Lost forever!

But if she had no human friends, Margret had Caliph who was wonderful company. And one day she had an adventure. That evening in bed she told her brothers and sister, "Imagine, I saw two ponies in town today."

"Ponies! Where?" the others cried excitedly. Even Matthias showed interest.

"Two sweet ponies," Margret told them, "almost as nice as Grandpa and Grandma's Tom and Tilly. Two steel-grey ponies just alike with long silky manes and tails. They were hitched to a small cart standing in the slaughter yard. Then the meat inspector came out with a little woman in a fur cap. He was carrying a whole tub full of meat scraps. 'There, now you can give your dogs a good meal again, Mrs. Almut,' he said. She gave me such a look, friendly as anything. Then she got upon the seat and the ponies trotted off. But before she came out I had a chance to pet the ponies and talk with them. I can hardly wait until next Friday to go back to the butcher, because I'm sure she comes every week."

Joey uttered a wail. "If only I didn't have that stupid old school I'd go with you."

"You'll have holidays at Christmas," Margret said. "Then I'll take you along, and if you save a piece of bread we'll give it to the ponies."

"Maybe," Joey said, already half asleep, "maybe the pony woman will be nice and let us have a little ride."

CHAPTER FOUR

A Sunday and Two Birthdays

MEANWHILE DECEMBER had come. At home that had always been the best month of the year, for the second of December was the twins' birthday and the ninth Andrea's. These three birthdays had always been celebrated together on the nearest Sunday of Advent.

The children always associated the fragrance of honey cake and the quiet glow of yellow tapers with the beginning of the Christmas season.

The night before the first Sunday of Advent Margret lay awake in her cold room thinking of many things. Her old Aunt Frederike used to say that Margret had been born under a lucky star. But it must have been Andrea who was. Things always went right for Andrea, and people always liked her. But nothing had gone right for Margret for a long time. She had felt cut in half since the death of Christian. She would never be whole again without her twin brother. How could being born under a lucky star help her?

Now she was fourteen years old. That was really quite grown up—at fourteen she felt she deserved a little respect from the younger ones. But instead Andrea seemed to be getting way ahead of her big sister. Nowadays Andrea was the important member of the family. She was always coming home from school with something new. It made Margret mind terribly about not being able to go to school herself. She was hungry for the things which could be found in books. Sometimes she would have a free half-hour and would get hold of a book and sit in the cold attic room reading with hot, flushed cheeks. But her happiest times were when Matthias borrowed a book from Dieter and read aloud to the family in the evening, while Mother sewed.

Margret loved those evenings when all of them listened to Matthias. Sometimes she and Matthias took turns doing a bit of translation from an American book. But these evenings were few and far between. Matthias was usually out somewhere with Dieter.

And now at last Dieter was to come to Parsley Street, for he had been invited to the birthday party. For weeks Margret had been saving flour and sugar and a tiny sliver of their butter ration for this great event, and she had saved enough for two big cakes.

Andrea had invited Lenchen, of course, and Joey's friend Hans Ulrich, too, was to be introduced to the family. Margret alone had nobody to invite. Finally she said, "You know, I'll invite Mrs. Verduz. She isn't my real friend, but she's actually quite nice and always so alone."

The family agreed, and so Mrs. Verduz was put down on the guest list.

Suddenly, in the midst of the consultations, Andrea exclaimed, "You keep inviting people and we have only five cups and each one different."

"We'll have our coffee first and then feed the company," Joey said.

"A fine way of doing things," Matthias said. "When you invite people you can't eat everything up first."

"Then we'll have to ask Mrs. Verduz to lend us dishes again." Mother sighed. The five cracked cups with broken handles came from Mrs. Verduz in any case.

"That'll be just fine," Andrea said happily. "Maybe she'll let us have the pretty set in the parlor with the gold rims and the forget-me-nots. I've always wanted to drink from those cups." And she offered to go downstairs to Mrs. Verduz at once, both to issue the invitation and bring up the matter of the dishes.

Advent morning came at last and Margret woke early. The first grey light of the winter day came in through the small window. Real cold had come early this year. On the walls of the room a thin layer of glittering ice crystals had formed. And everywhere in Germany people had little fuel to put in their stoves.

Margret sighed softly, sat up and kneeled for a long time in front of the mirror that hung above the bed. It was awful that she was not a bit pretty, she thought. Grey eyes, even a little greenish to be quite honest about it, with a darker ring around the iris. A straight-hanging mane of blond hair. Freckles on her nose. Not as many as Matthias, but still freckles. Who would ever look at a girl with freckles?

She got out of bed and went into the living room to the small tub at which the children washed. The ice cellar, which was what they called their bedroom, was too cold for washing, and in any case Mother thought it best to keep an eye on the process. It took a bit of pressing every morning to get Andrea and Joey to go through with it. Joey insisted that too much washing in winter was bad for the health. He had heard of a boy who got pneumonia from washing and died—or had come close to dying anyway.

This Sunday morning, when Margret entered the living room, her mother had the fire already started. The lamp was burning and beneath the lamp hung the Advent wreath—a real fresh green Advent wreath with four red candles. And what a lovely woodsy smell.

"Mummy," Margret cried. "An Advent wreath. Oh, Mummy, you're a magician. I always thought so."

"Yes," Mummy laughed, "who would have thought that I would be able to do magic with a needle. People do you all sorts of favors if you fix up their old clothes for them. But now wash up at the stove; there's warm water ready for you."

For Sunday breakfast there was the weekly butter ration for each member of the family, a tiny little square of butter which could either be eaten up at once or spread over several days. They had long done all their cooking without fats. After breakfast the whole family went to church, and then came the giving of presents. Presents? the girls asked in amazement; they thought they had heard wrong. Presents, just like in the good old days?

Yes, there were presents; there was even a birthday table, and it was so unexpectedly splendid that Margret and Andrea were dumbstruck. There were new dresses for the girls, each alike, made of heavy red material, with little white collars. Two new dresses—could such things still exist? It turned out that Mrs. Verduz had "found" the material in a cedar chest. Once the cloth had been a pair of curtains, but no one would ever have guessed that now.

Joey's present aroused as much admiration as the dresses. He had made bookmarks for each of the sisters. He made them of snippets of the red cloth prettily pasted on brown paper. These bookmarks would be very useful when they had some books again. "And look at the back," Joey told them.

He had done the back all by himself, without anyone to help him, and even the spelling was absolutely his own. There on the back of the bookmarks was HAPY BERTHDY in block letters that had been carefully cut out with a scissors and neatly pasted. The sisters thanked him again and again, and admired the presents prodigiously.

Matthias had made a little hand-written book with the words and music of all the old Christmas carols they used to sing at home. And somewhere he had obtained a beautiful apple for each of the sisters.

In the afternoon the girls put on their new dresses. They looked lovely. That particular shade of red was even becoming to Margret, who had always considered blue her color. Then the coffee table was set. It took a lot of pondering and giggling, for nine people were not going to fit very easily at the round table.

"Three on the sofa," Andrea reckoned. "More than three won't fit, no matter how skinny they are. And then six chairs all around. You'll have to go and borrow two more chairs, boys."

In fact everything was borrowed—the embroidered tablecloth, the gold-rimmed cups, and now two additional chairs.

But with the chairs around the table the effect was very festive indeed. Above the table hung the Advent wreath. Mother placed a few sprigs of pine among the cups, and on the middle of the table stood a plate heaped high with pieces of apple cake that made your mouth water.

If only the guests would come on time. But there was no need to worry about that. Before half past three the bell downstairs rang. Joey and Andrea rushed down together and ushered in their guests, Hans Ulrich and Lenchen. From innumerable swathings of paper Lenchen unwrapped a miracle. She had brought a cake studded with raisins—an unbelievable luxury—and dusted with glittering, snowy confectioner's sugar.

"Best regards from Mamma," Lenchen said, blushing deeply with embarrassment, "on account of the way you always help me so nicely."

Hans Ulrich stayed close to Joey, although he was ordinarily not shy. It was clear that he had washed for the solemn occasion within an inch of his life. His face gleamed and his hair was slicked down as if it had been ironed. Joey, who knew him only with a wild mop, looked at him askance.

Mother opened the conversation. "How old are you, Hans?" she asked. It turned out that Hans Ulrich had only the vaguest idea. "I might be seven," he offered.

"You ask your mother," Joey said.

"She doesn't know either. Anyway she isn't my right mother."

"But I'm sure she's good to you," Margret said quickly.

Hans Ulrich conceded that his foster mother was a good sport. In some ways she was better than most mothers because she did not worry over him and let him stay up as late at night as he liked. But he did not enjoy being sent out to the country to beg potatoes, especially not now that it was winter. On the other hand, snitching coal at the railroad station was fun.

Mrs. Lechow looked closer at the thin little boy with the roguish face, and decided to find out more about him.

The bell rang again. Matthias dashed downstairs to meet Dieter. At the same time there came a polite knock on the door and Mrs. Verduz entered, wearing her best grey silk dress which Mother had just recently redone for her. Caliph followed at her heels. And what was she carrying on a round platter? It was almost unbelievable—another cake!

Now that everyone was assembled, there was no need to postpone the refreshments. Everyone ate reverently, and the mountains of cake melted away without much talking.

"Do have another piece," Mother said, for Mrs. Verduz was the only guest who had to be urged. "I don't know whether I should," she replied, taking another piece of cake and placing it on her plate. "What marvelous apple cake, Mrs. Lechow—so crumbly and juicy . . ."

"It always turns out crumbly when you have to skimp on the shortening," Mother said. "Your cake is really remarkable, Mrs. Verduz." "Oh no, oh no." "Oh yes, oh yes! And the cake Lenchen's mother sent is very good, too. You haven't tried any of that yet." "I don't know whether I should," Mrs. Verduz replied.

Mother looked around the table. It was a joy to see so many happy faces.

"Gee, birthdays are nice," Hans Ulrich said, patting his stuffed belly.

"Will you invite me to yours?" Joey asked him.

"Can't. I don't have any."

"What do you mean? Everybody has a birthday."

"Not me. I don't know when it is, and nobody knows. I don't even have a family name."

They were all mystified at this. But Hans Ulrich explained it—the facts were very simple. He did not understand why the story should cause a sensation. That was just the way things were—what was there to look so grave about. Hamburg was a big city with lots of streets and towers and water. He remembered it only dimly. And then came the night when fire fell from Heaven and people screamed and his mother screamed too. She was put into a train, one with beds, and they rode very far. But when the train stopped his mother was no longer screaming and couldn't give her name or the child's name. All he knew how to say then was that he was Hans Ulrich. Perhaps Ulrich was his last name, perhaps his middle name. People guessed his age as about four. That had been in the summer of forty-three.

Everyone had fallen silent, and no more questions were asked. Margret lit the Advent candles and turned out the light. "Let's sing," Matthias said.

Dieter brought his guitar in from the hall. He tuned it, and Matthias tuned the violin; the girls and Mother bent their heads over the notebook and they all sang in pure, clear voices, *Come, All Ye Faithful*. The two boys played so beautifully that Hans Ulrich stared wide-eyed and Mrs. Verduz kept wiping the tip of her nose—she was so moved.

They sang all the old carols; they could not get enough of them. The candles burned brightly and the pine smelled sweet. Caliph lay on Margret's lap and purred.

"We're doing wonderfully," Dieter said. "We ought to get together and go out to the villages for carol singing."

The girls thought this was a wonderful idea. "Yes, yes, let's do that. We can, Mummy, can't we?"

"We'll see," Mother said cautiously.

Then they played parlor games, and Mrs. Verduz actually joined in and became quite gay and almost stopped looking stiff.

The climax of it all was when Hans Ulrich offered to eat a piece of cake while standing on his head.

"You're crazy," everyone cried. "It can't be done."

But Hans Ulrich was ready to prove that it could. Joey looked at the company triumphantly. This was the kind of friend he had.

Hans Ulrich took off his jacket, revealing a tattered and much-patched shirt. But everyone forgot about the shirt when he stood on his head as straight as a candle, while Joey fed one piece of cake after the next into his mouth. He chewed and actually swallowed, though his face turned beet-red and Mother was afraid he was going to choke. Everyone watched in respectful awe and applauded loudly.

Now Matthias too wanted to show off his friend. "Do a chickenyard, Dieter," he said. "You do it so well."

Dieter did not have to be coaxed. He instantly set up such a cackling and crowing and gabbling that even Caliph woke up and looked around with gleaming eyes. There were young cocks just learning to crow whose voices kept breaking, and a broody hen with a flock of peeping chicks, and finally a hen who had laid an egg and announced it to the world with joyous cackling. It was a wonderful perform-ance. When it was over and the storm of applause died down, Mother said that they must now finish up the cake. "I don't know whether I should," Mrs. Verduz said, and Andrea also said, "I don't know whether I should," because this seemed to her the height of gentility.

Then Mrs. Verduz's clock downstairs suddenly struck eight, to everyone's surprise, for it had only just been four. And they realized that in honor of the Sunday the electric light had not been turned off. The guests took their leave. They could be heard laughing and talking down the stairs and along Parsley Street, and then silence fell. But the family continued to chatter about all the events of this exciting day. Andrea could not stop; her cheeks glowed and her eyes shone gentian-blue above her red dress. Margret, who had been so merry all afternoon, became quiet and pensive. She was thinking about little Hans Ulrich, who did not even know his name. "Isn't his father still living?" she asked Joey. But how could Joey know. The father had been away in the army during the bombing of Hamburg. Hans Ulrich's picture had been published in the newspapers several times, but no one had come to claim him.

"Poor child," Mother said.

Joey shook his head vigorously. "He gets along good," he insisted. "He's more fun than anyone else in the class. Only he's pretty hungry most of the time. More than the rest of us. You know, Mummy, we ought to invite him here more often."

"Our rations aren't even enough for ourselves," Margret said.

"Never mind, you bring him along now and then," Mother said. "Where there are meals for five there'll always be a grain of corn for a sixth member of the flock."

CHAPTER FIVE

Hark, the Herald Angels

THE DIM December dawn was already seeping through the window, and still nobody in the whole house stirred! Joey stretched and pulled his short nightshirt down over his knees; it had got hitched up during sleep. Beside him he felt the hard, bony shape of his big brother. He moaned softly with impatience and snuggled up to Matthias. He was a shaggy Eskimo dog in an igloo on an icy Polar night. During the past few days Matthias had been reading the family one of Frithjof Nansen's books on exploring the Arctic. Gee, that was a swell book. Hans Ulrich and Joey had been discussing how old they would have to be to go on their first Polar expedition. "Wow," Joey said softly, trying to growl. There was a special knack to growling like a real husky. Dieter could do it. He could imitate any kind of animal: he could growl and bark, meow, whinny, moo and cackle. Dieter was marvelous, almost as marvelous as Matthias, and more fun. Only when he had them practicing singing he was stern and serious and hard to satisfy.

Gosh, how much they had practiced the past few weeks. And now the great day had come and they were going out to the villages to sing carols. If only the big ones didn't oversleep.

Joey's patience gave out. "Are you still asleep, Matthias?" he asked.

"Can't a man get a little rest on Sunday morning!" His brother growled like a bear whose winter sleep has been disturbed. Joey pounded his fists against the big bear's chest. It would be fun to have a little tussle. For a few minutes he passed the time playing bear-in-cave. It was a nice warm cave. Outside it was bitter cold. Cautiously, the bear cub lifted one leg and let a little of the outside air into the warm cave. Ouououou—it was cold. Then he blew small clouds with his breath. Maybe if he blew hard enough he could make snow clouds. Snow would go well with carol singing. On the other hand, if it snowed Mother probably would keep him home. He became hot all over at the thought. "Dear God, don't let it snow," he prayed, clasping his hands tightly. "Not until after we've started, but then let it snow like anything." He shouted the last word at the top of his voice so that God would be sure to hear.

"Now cut it out," Matthias thundered. "Making such a racket in the middle of the night! Have you gone out of your mind, twerp?"

"What can I do when I've been awake for hours?" Joey wailed. "You'll sleep the whole day away, you . . . you lazybones."

"Waking other people and then getting fresh besides!" Matthias said. "The nerve of you. If you're awake, get up quietly and go to the big room and wash up."

That was really insulting. "Wash!" Joey said. "Yesterday was Saturday night and Margret put me in the tub and scrubbed my skin right off."

"Out!" Matthias shouted.

"Go on, go in to Mother, you monster," a voice called from the girls' bed.

With a hearty push from behind, his big brother helped him out of bed. Freezing, he stood in the icy room, a wretched little figure. "Run," Margret called. "Otherwise you'll get a cold and sniffle all night so nobody can get to sleep."

He was already running. The floor was cold under his bare feet. Last night Matthias had carried him pickaback to bed and so he'd left his felt bedroom slippers in the other room. He pushed open the squeaky door into the hallway. This was a little warmer than the bedroom. He went on into his mother's room. Oh, the beautiful warmth of the big room. The stove was already hot and the room smelled of baked rolls. The frost flowers on the windows glistened moistly as they faded. And here at last he was greeted by a kind face and a friendly word. "Good morning, my baby," Mother said.

"Good morning, Mummy. Have you been up long? It must be nearly noon."

"It's just eight, darling."

"Then we'll have breakfast now and then lunch and then we'll go carol singing. Hurray!" Joey jumped on to the sofa and began bobbing up and down until the springs groaned. A pity her children had to work out their excess energy on the poor sofa. Mrs. Lechow thought. Luckily it was a good,

solid piece of furniture from way back when things were
made to last.

All sorts of sounds could be heard in the house now—the
squeaking of Mrs. Verduz's coffee grinder, the rattling of
dishes in her kitchen, her voice as she talked to Caliph. And
finally the sleepyheads in the next room began to stir. The
sisters came in, washed at the stove and put on their red Sunday dresses. Matthias, too, came in, and after breakfast he
sat around reading as though it were a perfectly ordinary
Sunday.

"When are we going?" Joey asked him for the hundredth
time.

"Around two," Matthias said.

"When will it be two?"

"My dear young man," Matthias said, "if you bother me
again there'll soon be one less Lechow in the world."

Not even dinner meant much to Joey, although Sunday
dinner included meat, two ounces for each of them, and
Margret had made potato dumplings and fine brown gravy.
But Hans Ulrich, who had arrived right on time for the
meal, did full justice to Margret's cooking.

While the girls were washing the dishes, Mother said to
Joey and Hans, "Get on your outside clothes, you two, and
go down and look for Dieter and Lenchen so they won't
have to ring. You know Mrs. Verduz takes a nap after lunch
on Sundays and doesn't like to be disturbed."

The two boys went down and stood sentinel in the hall.
They were already booted and spurred; as far as they were
concerned, the party could start out instantly. Joey was wearing the pants his mother had made out of an old woolen
blanket. They weren't exactly elegant, but they were warm

and large enough to allow for growth. Matthias had re-marked that the seat of those pants looked as if they were meant to fit a hippopotamus. Joey wasn't sure whether this was a slur or something to be proud of.

Happily, everything ends sometime, even the most boring wait. Dieter came punctually at two, carrying his carefully packed guitar, and a few minutes later Lenchen arrived, wearing a coat with a fur collar—awfully fancy, both boys thought. They were allowed to feel the fur, once each. Lenchen was a pleasure to have around anyway. She smelled so nicely of smoked meat, and her paper bag of provisions was delightfully full.

And so they started, started out at last! The two boys ran ahead, brimming over with excitement. They went past the old cemetery and the new cemetery to the outskirts of the city. This area had been badly bombed. The road went gradually uphill toward the last houses of the city, almost all of which were destroyed. Then it sloped down again toward a small pine forest and into a narrow valley with a little river and an old mill. The first village lay right across the river.

"We won't sing there," Dieter said. "It's too close to the town. The townsfolk come out here every day to beg for milk and potatoes. If we sing here, the farmers won't even listen."

A little beyond the village, on the highest point of the road, stood the Big Tower. The boys had often seen it from a distance. Now they studied the grey, round old structure and wondered what it was for. It had always been there. It was not as old as the mountains, but it was older than the oldest rowan tree along the road and the oldest people in the vicinity. Nobody knew of a time when it had not been there.

"It probably used to be a watch tower," Dieter said. "The robber knights used to look out over the country from such towers." But Hans Ulrich and Joey had already decided that it was the tower where Rapunzel had been locked up and from whose top window she had let down her golden hair for the prince to climb up by.

"Do you see Hellborn down there?" Matthias said. "That's where we're headed for, where the nice blacksmith lives who sold us our potatoes."

The first place they stopped to sing was a farm to the right of the road. Their voices sounded a little thin, as if they'd become rusted or frozen. An old woman came out of the barn, listened for a moment, then went back into the house and came out with an apron full of apples for them. That was a good beginning. They went on to the miller's. The place had a wonderful smell of gingerbread, and they sang there with a good deal more ease and zest. A window was opened and then closed again. They waited for a while, but nothing happened. At the blacksmith's farm they were disappointed to find all the windows dark. But the windows of the tavern across the road were cheerfully lit up. They went up to the door. Matthias peered in and drew back at once. "They're playing cards," he whispered to Dieter. Dieter shrugged. He knew that card-players did not like being disturbed. But the three girls and the two little boys looked hopeful and expectant; they thought everyone was longing to hear them sing.

"Let's start," Dieter said softly, giving the keynote. And they sang at the top of their voices, "God rest ye merry, gentlemen . . ."

It was a jolly tune. The tavernkeeper would surely come out and invite them into the warm room. Everybody inside would sit and listen, forgetting the card game. Of course, that was what would happen. And then, when the songs were over, perhaps the kindly innkeeper's wife would come out of the kitchen with apple cake for them all, or a tray of steaming cups of coffee, and muffins.

When, after their first song, no invitation to come in was offered, Matthias opened the door himself, and somewhat hesitantly they all filed into the tavern. A green tile stove poured out heat. Cards slapped on the table. No one looked up. Dieter raised his arm and they began singing what was their liveliest tune:

> *Good King Wenceslas looked out*
> *On the Feast of Stephen*
> *When the snow lay round about*
> *Deep and crisp and even.*
> *Silver shone the moon that night,*
> *Though the cold was cruel,*
> *When a poor man came in sight*
> *Gath'ring winter fuel.*

Never had they sung it so well, they thought. One of the men at the rear table looked up and gave the children a friendly nod. When they sang the second verse,

> *"Hither, page, and stand by me,*
> *If thou know'st it telling,*
> *Yonder peasant, who is he?*
> *Where and what his dwelling?"*
> *"Sire, he lives a good league hence,*
> *Underneath the mountain,*
> *Right against the forest fence,*
> *By Saint Agnes' fountain,"*

there was a moment of silence in the room. Then, slap! a card was thrown down on the table. "That takes it," one of the men shouted, and the loud talk and laughter began again.

"Come," Dieter said, running his hand over Hans Ulrich's and Joey's heads. "They've never heard of Christmas here."

The group shuffled slowly out of the door. The tavern-keeper, who had been sitting half asleep behind the counter, appeared to notice them for the first time. He fumbled in a drawer, took out a one-mark note and handed it to Dieter. "There y'are. Now go on and don't bother people. We only sing in church around here."

"Thank you," Dieter said, and let the crumpled bill flutter back onto the counter.

Outside it was already growing dark, and from the grey mass of clouds overhead a few sparse snowflakes began falling.

"It's snowing," Andrea cried, taking little skips. "Now we'll have a real Christmas."

The wind was sharper than it had been and the blue wall of mountains in the distance looked gloomy and threatening. The two little boys had become very quiet. They had expected carol singing to be much jollier.

"Look, Joey, it's snowing," Margret said. "You kept wishing it would."

"Yes," Joey said, a faint quaver in his voice.

A side road led into the woods. In a little clearing stood a small shed from which a faint light gleamed. Next to it was a sheepfold. A dog began barking and a rumbling voice called out, "Who's there?"

Inside the fence the sheep were crowding together, a grey mass of woolly backs smelling of animal warmth. The shepherd came out of the shed, looked at the children and softly called back his shaggy dog. Growling, the dog lay down at his feet. The children began to sing:

> *The holly and the ivy,*
> *Wherever they are grown,*
> *Of all the trees that are in the wood*
> *The holly takes the crown.*
> *The blowing of the horn,*
> *And the running of the deer*
> *And the pealing of the merry organ,*
> *Sweet singing in the choir.*

The shepherd stood still, leaning on his staff. The dog stopped growling and swept his bushy tail gently back and forth, his eyes fixed on his master's face.

"That was pretty," the shepherd said. "Sing me another."

How glad they were to be asked. They sang their *Good King Wenceslas* again, and then *Hark, the Herald Angels Sing*.

The shepherd nodded and beckoned to them to come into the shed, for the snow was falling more thickly now. Inside, a lantern hung on the wall and a fire was burning in the crude fireplace, above which a battered kettle hung. In one corner was a bed, and on the other side of the hut a pile of hay.

"Sit down," the shepherd said. Now, by the light of the lamp, they saw that he was a very old man. His beard had more white in it than grey; a pair of bushy eyebrows stood like two grey thatched roofs above his bright eyes. It seemed to the children that they had suddenly stepped out of space and time and entered the Holy Land of two thousand years ago.

Lenchen, practical little person that she was, returned first to reality. She unpacked her sandwiches and passed them around. The shepherd, too, was given one. Silently, they ate. The dog lay down by the fire and blinked sleepily at them.

"Where are you from?" the old man asked.

"From the city," Matthias said. "We wanted to go carol singing."

"People around here don't know the custom— Here, have an apple." From a box he took a number of beautiful ruddy apples and gave them to the children. "That's all I have. Where are you going from here?"

"To the farm on the right there, beyond the woods."

"You'll do better to go up the hill and then take the road that goes off to the left of the highway. They ain't so well off as they used to be at Rowan Farm, but Mrs. Almut is the kind that always has something left over for others. And she likes singing, I know that."

Mrs. Almut, Margret thought. Where have I heard that name before?

"And now sing me one more," the shepherd said. "Time passes slowly when you're all alone out here. But the sheep can always find something to eat along the sides of the road and in the woods as long as the snow isn't too deep."

They sang:

The first Noel the angels did say
Was to certain poor shepherds in fields as they lay;
In fields where they lay keeping their sheep
On a cold winter's night that was so deep.
Noel, Noel, Noel, Noel,
Born is the King of Israel.

"Now good-by, and thank you very much," the old man said to them. And as they filed out they heard him remark to his dog, "Well, boy, we don't often have the angels come and sing to us like the shepherds at Bethlehem." The big dog wagged his tail softly.

Outside the pines and hemlocks were already wearing white caps. Above on the hill, through the trees, they could see a single light. "That's Rowan Farm," the shepherd called after them.

The carolers tramped through the snow. The woods were full of Christmas trees. The branches crackled softly and the forest seemed enchanted, full of strange shapes, white gnomes and witches, hooded and mysterious figures. An owl wailed out its long, questioning cry. Hans Ulrich and Joey held each other's hands tightly. When they came out of the woods the wind blew snow into their faces and the snowflakes stung like thousands of little pinpricks. "This must be the way to the farm," Dieter said when they reached a stone bench upholstered all in white. "I saw the light glimmering right there behind that group of trees. Say, what's that? Sounds like a whole pack of dogs."

As they approached the farm the noisy barking of several dogs grew louder. The lights of the house shone clearly now. A low stone wall encircled the farmyard. One side of the yard was bounded by the barn, and a high gate closed the entrance into the farmyard. They could see the dark figures of big dogs leaping up against the fence of a kennel.

Margret ran ahead to the gate to see the dogs. The others heard her shout, "Come quick, they're Great Danes!" She began talking to them in a low, affectionate voice as she never talked to people. She had not seen a Great Dane since the death of their own dog, Cosi.

"Better bring her back, Matthias," Andrea said. "Or else she'll be spending the night with them." And Margret was calling, "There are *three* of them, Matthias, look, look. Yes, I know you're barking, but it's not because you don't like us, you beauties, you just have to keep watch."

"Come along, Margret," Matthias called. "We have to go in. It's getting pretty late and Mother will worry."

He opened the gate that led to the house, and they entered the yard. Light streamed from the windows of the house so that the yard itself was lit up. They took up their posts in front of the door and started singing:

> *Hark, the herald angels sing*
> *Glory to the newborn King;*
> *Peace on earth and mercy mild,*
> *God and sinners reconciled . . .*

A shadow crossed the lamplight, a face appeared at the window and vanished again. Then the front door opened and a small woman looked out. "The pony woman!" Margret cried out.

The woman laughed. "Come on in," she said cordially.

Margret was no sooner inside the door than she noticed that the house was not a typical farmhouse. The large hallway contained some old, heavy, highly polished pieces of furniture. There was an old grandfather clock, a dark oak table, some high-backed chairs with rush seats. The door to one of the rooms was open, and while the singers were stamping the snow from their boots a huge beast, the color of a lion, rose from a sheepskin rug by the stove and walked slowly toward them. Lenchen and the two boys retreated behind Matthias and Dieter.

"It's all right, Fury," the woman said. A look of ecstasy had come over Margret's face. "Another one!" she exclaimed happily, and she held out her hands for the dog to sniff. The big head came closer and the tail began wagging. Margret placed her hand on the dog's head. He seemed to have no objection and stood there, close beside her, while the group sang through the many verses of *The Twelve Days of Christmas.*

There was a spinning wheel in the room to which they had been led. It stood beside the tile stove—not as an ornament, but as a useful tool, and now the pony woman went back to it. The low hum of the wheel made an accompaniment to their song. The doors to the hall had been left open, and the children noticed that more doors kept opening in the quiet house and more ears were listening to their singing. They sang all their songs over again; they felt as if they could go on singing forever.

A lamp was burning brightly behind a parchment shade with a pattern of delicate grasses. The walls and ceiling of the room were a light greyish blue, like the color of the sky on the first day of spring. And the woman's dress was blue also, with a snowy collar. The eyes in her tanned face shone like two small, warm suns. She had dark, close-cropped hair shot through with grey threads like a silvery web.

"Kathrin," she called when the children had finished their songs. "There's plenty of potato salad left," she said to the children. "And Kathrin will make some hot coffee. What do you say to that?"

No one had any objections. They sat down around the

large table. An old peasant woman came shuffling out of the kitchen and set plates, cups and a huge flowered stoneware bowl full of potato salad on the table. The lady of the house whispered something to her; she shook her head disapprovingly but went back to the kitchen and reappeared shortly with a steaming pot of coffee and a plate heaped with slices of sausage.

"Hurrah!" Hans Ulrich cried out, and instantly gagged his mouth with his hand; the sight of the sausage had been too much for him. The little lady laughed so that her whole face became a maze of jolly wrinkles. Then she said, "Well, pitch in."

They ate silently and reverently. The potato salad even had some bacon in it. But, alas, they weren't able to eat it all, because Lenchen's sandwiches were too recent. One after the other they said their thank yous. A handsome white-haired old man came out of one of the rooms and looked them over in a kindly way. "I should like to thank you," he said courteously, smiling at each of them. "You have given me great pleasure with your beautiful singing."

Margret had slipped up close to Mrs. Almut. She still had something on her mind. She asked it the first chance she had. "Please, may I see the other dogs?"

"Come along," the pony woman said. "I have to go out to feed them anyhow. That's my last chore of the day. I don't have a kennel maid. It's funny, the country girls don't want to have anything to do with raising dogs; most of them don't like animals at all. And you wouldn't catch a city girl coming out here where we're so isolated, with no movie theaters for miles around."

Margret followed her across the yard. From one of the

barns came a soft, contented mooing. They took a quick look in at the horse stable where the two handsome greys were contentedly munching their oats. The ponies instantly raised their heads and began nibbling tenderly at Mrs. Almut's sleeve. "This is Mimi," Mrs. Almut said, patting the mare's neck. "I hope she'll foal in the summer."

"A colt!" Margret exclaimed. "Might I come out here after it's born and see it?"

"Of course you may. But now we'd better feed those beasts. They know I'm out here; hear the racket they're making."

Between the horse stable and the cowbarn a small door led to the dogs' kitchen where the scrap meat was cooked. On her own initiative Margret took one of the big knives and helped cut up the steaming lumps of meat that Mrs. Almut ladled out of the kettle. Four big bowls were standing ready, but only two ladlefuls of meat were placed in each. The dogs got only a small feeding at night, Mrs. Almut said.

As they crossed the yard with the bowls, the huge animals leaped up against the gate that partitioned off their part of it, and barked loudly. Fury had come out also, but he trotted alongside with a rather bored look.

"Aren't you at all scared?" Mrs. Almut asked. Margret only shook her head; she could scarcely wait to get into the kennel. The dogs danced around them; they took hold of their mistress' skirt and pulled her toward the stand where their bowls were set down. Fury alone had to be invited. "You have to coax him," Mrs. Almut said. "These big hounds are often like that, the worst eaters."

The dogs stood in the full light of the kitchen window while they gobbled their food. "The big dam is wonderful,"

Margret said. "And I think the lighter of the two puppies is going to turn out something special."

"Well, well, so you know something about great Danes?" the woman said.

"We used to have a wonderful dam at home. We raised a couple of litters from her. My mother always took me to the dog shows when there was one in the neighborhood, and once I went to the big show in Berlin."

"Is that so? Well— The lighter one is named Alf. He's sold already. To an American captain who'll be coming for him soon. Four weeks ago his hindquarters looked rather poor so that I did not want to keep him for breeding."

"I wouldn't let him go for anything," Margret said. "He's really too good to be sold."

"Then you think he'll turn out better than his brother? You know, I've thought so myself recently. They're six months old now—it's so hard to tell about them at that age."

They started walking back to the house. Margret thought, now I must ask her, now or never. If only her heart wouldn't pound so. But finally she brought out the question. "If you really need a kennel maid, couldn't I—couldn't you take me?"

The pony woman laughed. "How old are you anyway, you funny girl who comes down the road and gives me pointers on my dogs?"

"I'll be fifteen," Margret said—quite truthfully; after all, she wasn't being asked *when* she would be fifteen.

"Child, you have no idea what the job involves. I can't afford to have a girl for the dogs alone. She would have to milk and take a hand in everything. Kathrin is old and can't do very much any more and I'm always up to my neck in work."

"I see," Margret said sadly. Of course Mrs. Almut wouldn't want her; that would have been too good to be true.

"The last girl I had threw up the job after a month," Mrs. Almut went on. "I couldn't really blame her for it. She had taken up stenography in school and had the best marks in her class, but the Labor Office had to send the poor thing out to work in a barn. They said there were no openings for office workers. But the daughter of our local mayor, who was brought up in the country, still lives here and can't type worth a cent, goes into town to work in an office and thinks herself quite a lady because she can keep her fingernails painted."

"Oh yes," Margret said. She knew the Labor Office. "But, please, won't you think it over, please, won't you? You see, I'm much stronger than I look, really I am. My name is Margret Lechow and I live at Thirteen Parsley Street."

Her voice was so imploring that Mrs. Almut did not have the heart to tell her no. "We'll see," she said.

All the way home Margret kept thinking about it. For a while she would be filled with wild hopes. Then she would pull herself up short. Something so good could never come true. The ponies and the dogs! They had let her stroke them right away. No, there was no use letting yourself dream impossible things. If a good fairy had come and said: you can have three wishes. . . . Well, she knew what the first two of them would be, because she had wished them for years, but the third would certainly be to be allowed to go out to Rowan Farm and work for the pony woman as kennel maid.

Joey was clinging to her hand and trudging along beside her in the darkness. "Is it far to home?" he asked once or twice. Hans Ulrich, too, was plainly tired, although he did not say a word about it. And even Andrea and Lenchen were surprised at how much longer the walk home was than the walk out had been. When they came to the woods near Hellborn, the wind cut icily through their clothes. There were no stars in the sky, and even the trees along the road moaned softly from cold.

Matthias was carrying a plump round sausage in his ruck-sack, and a bottle of milk. That was Rowan Farm's payment for the caroling. "I am going to cut it up into a fair share for all," he said. But Hans Ulrich said, "I'd sooner have a piece of it at your house, when the rest of you eat yours." And Lenchen would not take a share; at home she had all the sausage she wanted. Dieter, too, said he didn't need a share.

"My friend Hans and the boys have been doing some trucking for the miller in Dittmark. His barn needed roofing and they've been helping out. He paid them their wages in food. So we're pretty well stocked up now."

"What boys are you talking about?" Matthias asked in amazement.

"Oh, that's right, you don't know about the changes in our household," Dieter said. "You know the young fellows we saw so often in the café. Well, two of them have moved in with us. We had the devil of a time getting residence permits for them, so they could stay in the city legally. But the Youth Warden helped us out with that. Both the boys are musical, and we're practicing every free hour we have. But that's only half the story. We've got two more besides them. There have been six of us for nearly a week now."

"Tell us about them, Dieter," Margret said.

"Well, it was like this," Dieter began. Last week he'd been near the railroad station and two young fellows had approached him, wanting a handout. They looked pretty cold and pinched. There were jobs waiting for them in another city, they said, but they didn't have the fare. Dieter didn't fall for that story. He started questioning them in a friendly way and soon found out what was up. The two boys had made a good living on the Black Market all summer and fall, but they'd never had a place to live, had spent their nights in the waiting rooms of railroad stations, or camping out. But now it was cold and they'd been having no luck with their "business." They, too, had no identity papers, of course, and were in dread of being picked up by the police. They were thoroughly miserable. The older one, it turned out, had a year's training as an automobile mechanic. The younger one said he was a musician.

"Oho," Matthias said, grinning.

Dieter cleared his throat. "What else could I do?" he said. "I took them along home."

"Just like you," Matthias growled. "They might have cleaned you out, too."

"We weren't born yesterday either. They tried it, but we lit into them good and then . . ."

"Then?" all three girls asked at once.

Dieter laughed with a trace of embarrassment. "Well, we let them stay anyway."

"There's nobody like you, Dieter!" Andrea exclaimed.

"We've known that all along," Matthias said.

"You'd have to have a heart of concrete to turn those kids out on the street in these below-zero days. You would have kept them, too. And the two of them are really all right. All they need is someone who'll give them a good shaking and talking-to. You should have seen their faces when we played for them. Tim is nineteen and Axel, the one who calls himself a musician, is seventeen, and neither of them had ever heard a Mozart sonata. I had a long talk with the pastor's wife about the case. She's going to help me soften up the Youth Warden so he'll give them a break. Both the fellows are sick to death of drifting around without a home."

"I should think so," Matthias said. "They'd much prefer moving in with you and letting you feed them."

"Feed them? That wouldn't get them anywhere. Don't worry about that, they have to put in a day's work, just like the other two. As a matter of fact, Hans can use them, and they've been working hard. Evenings we go in for music. We're planning to get up a little orchestra."

"So you're going to tame them with music," Matthias grinned.

By now the snow was falling faster and faster. The whole world seemed to be wrapped in fleecy wool. "How far is it to home?" Joey asked again.

At last they saw the first lights of the city. And then it wasn't long before they saw the glowing gable window in Parsley Street where Mother was waiting for them.

CHAPTER SIX

Fear Not

"Is it Christmas yet?" Joey asked his big brother the first thing when he got up in the morning. Normally Joey stayed sound asleep when Matthias got up at six and groped for his clothes in the dark. But these days Joey was always up early.

"Tomorrow," Matthias said on the Monday after their carol singing. This hour in the morning he never felt particularly good-humored. "Go back to sleep, squirt. Little boys who don't get enough sleep stop growing."

"I am sleeping. Is tomorrow far away?"

"Twenty-four hours. And then another twelve hours until evening."

"It won't ever come," Joey groaned and pulled the blanket up over his nose.

Matthias went in his stocking feet to the big room where Mother had already made coffee for him. He always felt sorry that she had to get up so early on his account. If only it had been possible to buy a thermos bottle she could have made the coffee the night before. Of course he could have

made the coffee himself; there was nothing to it. But on
weekdays the stove was not started until later in the day, or
their slender supply of wood would never have lasted. And
the electric current was usually turned off by six in the morning, so that the hot plate had to be switched on before six in
order to boil water for coffee. Once Mother had made the
coffee and placed the pot under the cosy to keep warm, she
usually slipped back into bed. There was nothing much you
could do in the dark and cold of early morning.

An end of a candle was burning on the table. Curled
under the feather bed, Mother looked like a little girl, Matthias thought. Her dark, loosened hair made a small cloud
around her thin face. She smiled at him. Every morning he
was greeted by this smile. It alone was almost enough to
warm him. He sat down facing her and crumbled the dry
bread into the steaming coffee. The room was still faintly
warm from last night, but the windows glittered with hoar-
frost.

Those few minutes alone with his mother early in the
morning, when his brother and sisters were still asleep, held
a quiet beauty for Matthias. At such times Mother discussed
everything with him and he realized that in spite of being
only fifteen he was the man of the house. "How are our
potatoes holding out?" she would ask him. Or, "Where in
the world can we get wood? If we aren't able to heat the
room I won't be able to sew, and the welfare alone isn't
enough to live on."

"Don't worry," Matthias said with a grown-up, confident
air. "The construction job stops for the whole of Christmas
week. I'll be able to go out to Rowan Farm with Dieter and
chop wood. The pony woman said that if we did some chop-

ping for her in her woodlot, we could have some wood for ourselves. And she'll give us our meals, too, while we're working there."

"She seems to be a very nice person."

"She certainly is. And she's glad to get someone to chop wood for her; it's too hard a job for her old hired man to do alone."

"But I was hoping you'd be able to get some rest during Christmas week, Matthias. You ought to have a chance to catch up on sleep."

"I'll get some extra sleep during the holidays. It's fun going out with Dieter anyhow. Maybe one of his gang will come along, and then we'll get a lot done in one day."

He chewed the last bit of bread, pulled his cap over his ears and donned his canvas gloves. "So long," he said. His mother pulled his head down and he rubbed his face against her cheek. Of course that was something he could do only when he was alone with her; it wouldn't do to let the youngsters see him getting soft. Her face was so small; how had this frail little woman got all of them through the hardships of the past three years? All, that is, but one.

Matthias walked softly down the steps, opened the cellar door and took his shoes from the shelf. Sitting on the lowest step of the stairs, he put on his heavy clodhoppers. Then he went out the front door, locked it from outside again, and pocketed the key. A man who went to work early in the morning had to have a key of his own—even Mrs. Verduz had recognized that.

Parsley Street was grey in the dawn of an icy December day. Only a few windows were dimly lit. The electricity was off now and not many people had candles or kerosene lamps.

Those who did not have to go to work lay abed as long as possible in order to save light and heat.

Matthias turned up his jacket collar and drew in his head. It was frightfully cold. Lucky his cap had earflaps. He tried to whistle. The best thing you could do was to take your mind off how cold you were. He would not have minded it if his work gave him any pleasure. The other day Dieter was talking about the students in Frankfurt and Marburg, whose classrooms were unheated and who were hungry and cold all the time, who had no books or material for experiments and had to work after school hours too. But at least they were doing what they wanted to do, Matthias thought. They saw a goal and a future. That made it easier for them.

Dieter was at the corner waiting for him. Every morning they met here and walked to work together. Their last construction job had been building a garage for the American occupation troops, and the Americans had supplied them with a warm meal at noon—and what a meal! But that was over. Now they were repairing a bombed warehouse. The old bricks which lay around in huge heaps had to be cleaned off and used for interior walls. Mixing the mortar, running back and forth with bricks for the cleaners and the masons, smoothing off the finished walls so that the stucco could be laid on—all these jobs fell to the apprentices and unskilled workers like Matthias and Dieter.

"But don't think this time has been for nothing," Dieter said to Matthias that noon. "I've made a point of working for all sorts of craftsmen for a few months at a time—masons, carpenters and once even a glazier. You'd be surprised how handy all that came in when Hans and I fixed up our cellar last summer. The thing is to keep your eyes open and learn something from all the jobs. Sooner or later it will come in useful."

"As long as you're around it isn't half bad."

"And don't forget you've got that wonderful mother of yours and a home, though it isn't exactly palatial, and all the youngsters. And you're getting on better on the job, too, aren't you? All you have to do is learn how to stick up for yourself. The fellows aren't bad; they just like to get your goat. It's the same everywhere. And not half bad compared to the army."

"Didn't you like being a soldier?"

"When I think of the way they took us for a ride, I still feel as if I could smash everything in sight. Only smashing things never made anything any better. When I was sixteen they set me to ditchdigging on the West Wall. A sea of mud and enemy planes overhead. A rotten deal, and I knew it. At home we never cared much for all the heiling and hurrahing."

"Your folks, too?" Matthias asked in amazement. "I always thought my folks were the only ones who weren't all out for the government. There was a while when I actually felt ashamed of them."

"Better than having to feel ashamed now. Where was I— Oh yes, they had me working on the West Wall, and then I came home and our house was gone. It's a queer feeling when you stand on the spot and nothing is left of what used to be there, just the broken walls, and none of the people. . . . Then later they took me into the army. They gave us a graduation certificate when they took us, but now it doesn't count for anything. So after all we've been through they tell us we'll have to go back to school again. But how can we gain admission to one of the crowded universities? Even if they'd take us, what would we do about the tuition fees? You can't make enough working, and I just wasn't cut out to be a Black Marketer."

"Then aren't you going to try to study music?"

"No, I'm giving up that idea. What's the use of aiming too high. These past few weeks I've thought it all over. After all, there are six of us living in the cellar now. It's time we started on a serious project. We sound all right as a dance band— I've heard a lot worse—and we've already had some offers from restaurants. The boys have been practicing song numbers, too. What we've got to do is write a few good cabaret songs and a peppy melody that's got rhythm and style and just a dash of bitter-sweet—that's what people want nowadays. I have to get going on that now, for myself and for the rest of the boys. That's why I'm quitting the construction job the first of January."

Matthias did not speak; he felt as if he had been hit with a club. Quitting the construction job, Dieter had said. What about himself? How was he going to stand it now?

Work on the job was supposed to be finished at noon on December twenty-fourth. But it was nearly three o'clock before Matthias and Dieter were through with all the cleaning up and collecting tools. As they went home together, Matthias was still choking back his unhappiness. He felt so bad that he didn't even look forward to Christmas and his few days off.

At the corner of Parsley Street Dieter slapped him on the back. "Well, old man, when are we going out to Rowan Farm to chop wood?"

"I guess I'll go alone," Matthias growled.

"Go alone? When did you get that idea?"

"When?" Matthias said, kicking the innocent wall of a building with his heavy shoe. "If you think I can stand being alone on that rotten job, I can stand chopping wood alone."

Dieter stood with his hands thrust deep into his pockets, the wind blowing his hair over his forehead. He brushed it back, shook his head and looked at Matthias with that warm smile of his that was almost impossible to resist. "But, Mat, we'll go on being friends, job or no job. That's settled. Isn't it? Well, then? Right after Christmas, eh?"

Matthias nodded. "Bring your ax along. You'd better put a good edge on it first. Oh, and I wanted to ask you, will you have time to drop in on us during the holidays?"

"Of course. Tomorrow we're playing at the Burg Café, and the day after we have an engagement at an office party. Good pay and free meals besides. The boys are all excited about it, because it's our first engagement. But I'll come over on the afternoon of the twenty-sixth. What's the little fellow, Hans Ulrich, doing for. Christmas?"

"He's coming to our house. His foster mother was invited out to some friends in the country and didn't know what to do with him. You know what that funny kid said? 'I'm in luck again,' he said. 'If she'd taken me with her I couldn't have visited with you.'"

They laughed. "What a kid," Dieter said. "So long, Matthias." And he walked off down the street, taking long strides, his hands in his pockets and his head bare to the wind.

The children sat in the dark, cold bedroom while their mother lit the Christmas tree in the other room.

All day long the girls had worked cleaning and making

everything in the house festive. They had polished Mrs. Verduz's old furniture until it shone and decorated the rooms with pine branches. Then Mother had sent them out to deliver Christmas packages to the old Lebenows, to the Millaus and to Mrs. Krikoleit. "You can't be so poor that you have nothing to give for Christmas," Mother had said. The gifts were only little nothings, a kerchief made out of a remnant of cloth, a pair of children's slippers, an embroidered bib for the baby. But how much joy these little gifts gave. Everywhere the women had tried to make their wretched dwellings a bit festive for Christmas Eve, to dress up the greyness of everyday life with a few twigs of pine. But nobody, the girls thought, had done as well as Mother in creating a real Christmas mood, that wonderful atmosphere compounded of expectation, hope and a warm, quiet joyousness of the heart.

Now they sat in the dark room, and that too was a part of Christmas. Joey and Hans Ulrich could hardly sit still. Could there really be candles for the little tree? And could Mother have baked cookies? Sure enough, there had been good smells in the house, but the fragrance might have come from Mrs. Verduz's kitchen. Probably the American relatives had sent Mrs. Verduz the materials. What the children did not know was that for weeks Margret had been battling with her mother over their ration stamps. "How can I cook if you rob me of everything to use for the holidays?" Margret had complained again and again. "You've taken all the sugar and a week's ration of fat and what little meat we get from every one of our cards."

"Oh well," her mother had answered, "it's worth scrimping a bit now if we can live in luxury over the holidays."

"It won't be luxury anyway, and if we save out everything for three weeks we'll be hungry as bears."

"You always are, you wolf cubs."

"Wolf cubs can't be hungry as bears Mummy, it's a zoological paradox," Margret said sternly. "And besides you have no sense of responsibility. Heaven only knows what you have in mind. Anyway, you're ruining my whole menu plan."

"Plans are made to be ruined," Mother said, and then she laughed so infectiously that Margret had to laugh with her.

There was no Christmas bell such as they had had at home, but outside the great bells of the church rang through the cold winter night, and Mother stood at the open door and sang softly, "Now come ye, Oh children all."

Hans Ulrich and Joey almost tumbled over themselves as they shot out of one room and into the next. There stood the tree with its four white candles shining like a starlit sky. There was even a little angel's-hair draped over the green twigs which gave out so sweet a scent of woods and Christmas. A snow-white cloth covered the table, and on it stood a plate of cookies, brown, crumbly spice cookies. And under the tree lay a present for everybody. Really princely presents. There were heavy knit gloves for the three boys— no one could imagine where Mummy had found the wool. Margret kept looking at the gloves; they reminded her of something. Then she suddenly remembered that she had once had a pair of ski socks just that color—but surely there had been nothing left of those socks but holes. And for the girls there were two gay hats, each with a long tassel, and a muffler to match, Andrea's red and Margret's grass green. Mother had earned the wool by doing sewing for people.

The presents lay there in the candlelight. They could be looked at but not touched; this was too solemn a moment. First the Christmas carols had to be sung, and the children could sing like angels, Dieter had said. It seemed as though the whole old house were listening, and perhaps in truth the house had never heard such sweet and lovely singing.

Then Andrea read aloud the Christmas story, as one of the children had always done at home on Christmas Eve. Everyone listened in complete silence, and for them it was not a distant and strange event that Mary had had to lay her son down in a manger because people turned her away from their doors and because there was no room in all of Bethlehem. More than once they themselves had known a baby to be born on the highway or in a stable, or in a cattle car rolling across the countryside in the dead of winter. The Christmas story was dearer and more familiar to them, perhaps, than it had ever been before to children in all the world's past. They knew poverty, cold and homelessness, they knew the warm breath of animals in a stable which alone makes an icy night friendlier and milder. And they knew, too, the bright glitter of the stars on wintry nights. The Christ Child was like a little brother to them, near and dear, as though they themselves had seen His mother hold Him close against her to keep Him from freezing. Breathlessly they listened to Andrea's voice as she read:

"And the angel said unto them: Fear not: for behold, I bring you good tidings of great joy which shall be to all people. For unto you is born this day in the city of David a Saviour, which is Christ the Lord."

Andrea stood reverently with the light of the candles

shimmering in her wide-open eyes and gleaming on her red Sunday dress.

"And suddenly there was with the angel a multitude of the heavenly host praising God and saying, Glory to God in the highest, and on earth peace, good will toward men."

Mother stood very still beside the tree, buried in thought for a moment. "Fear not," she thought, and Margret felt as if she could read her mother's thoughts and said to herself, "Fear not!"

All of a sudden there was a small noise at the door, and when they turned, Mrs. Verduz was silently slipping into the room, saying, "I don't know whether I should, Mrs. Lechow, if I'm really not in the way . . ."

"Why of course not," Mother said. "And Merry Christmas to you. We're so glad you've come."

"Don't you have any tree?" Joey asked.

"Oh, it isn't worth while just for me," Mrs. Verduz said. "I don't usually make any fuss over Christmas. But when I heard you singing I thought it was really awfully dull staying down there in my room all by myself. And you see, I've brought a few things with me."

And what wonders were placed under the tree now. A schoolbag with sealskin straps for Joey, a real good old-fashioned one. And for each of the others a book from the collection of Mrs. Verduz's late husband. There was even a book for Hans Ulrich. It was called *The Treasure in the Cellar* and it had a marvelous bright-colored jacket. Hans Ulrich held on to it tightly all evening, and during supper he sat down on it so that nobody could take it away. Maybe learning how to read wasn't so pointless.

Then Matthias went down and brought up the little cabi-

net that he and Dieter had made for Mother. It fitted perfectly into the corner by the window, so that as soon as it
was in place Mother wondered how she could possibly have
got along without it.

"It's from us, too," Joey said, pounding first himself and
then Hans Ulrich on the chest. "We helped too, didn't we,
Matthias?"

"Yes," Matthias said. "We never would have got it done
without your help."

Andrea had knitted potholders from cotton yarn which
had obviously once been white. And she had earned the
yarn herself; Lenchen's mother had given her a bundle of it
for regularly helping Lenchen with her homework.

Margret had racked her brains to think of something she
could give Mother, but there was nothing she could buy and
so she had finally decided to write a poem for her. She had
written it down in her best handwriting on a white sheet of
paper that Mrs. Verduz gave her, and painted pine twigs
with bright candles and yellow stars all around as a border.
She gave it to her mother who understood at once that it was
not meant for the public, but for herself alone.

The report cards of Andrea, Joey and Hans Ulrich, on the
other hand, were very much public property. As a surprise
they had saved all their report cards for this evening and
not mentioned them to a soul. To Joey the most wonderful
part of it was receiving a report card at all. It was the first
one in his whole life.

After supper Mother sat down under the tree—they had
blown out the candles so that they could be lit again—and
read the report cards aloud. Andrea, the oldest of the three,
came first. Her report read:

German: very good. Religion: very good. English: **very** good. Arithmetic: satisfactory. Sewing: deficient.

"I don't see why I got deficient when I made those beautiful potholders," Andrea contended. "Lenchen didn't think it was a fair mark either."

Still it was the only Deficient on Andrea's report card. She had good marks in all her other subjects. Under Conduct there was a note from her teacher: "Andrea is often restless during class. Her interest should be more regular; she also ought not to chatter so much. Her trouble is too much imagination and too little steadiness."

"Now it's my turn," Joey clamored. And then Mummy read out: "Arithmetic: deficient. Writing: satisfactory. Reading: satisfactory."

"You see," Joey said, looking around the circle with a beaming smile.

"Arithmetic deficient," Matthias reminded him.

"Yes, but that's better than Unsatisfactory."

"Gym: very good," Mummy read.

"That's the best mark you can get."

And under Conduct was written: "Joseph is apt to get restless during class. In the schoolyard his wild conduct often gives cause for complaint. He must learn to stop tussling with other boys. With some effort he will still be able to come up to the class standard. On the whole he has too much imagination and too little perseverance."

"Amazing," Mother said, turning her eyes from blond Joey to dark-haired Andrea. "And people sometimes say that there is no such thing as family resemblances. And now you, Hans Ulrich."

With modest pride Hans Ulrich handed over his card. It

read almost exactly like Joey's, point for point, except that
in penmanship he had a deficient instead of satisfactory.
And under Conduct was the comment: "Hans Ulrich must
show much more effort if he is to reach the class standard."

"Show effort, infant," Matthias said, giving him a paternal
pat on the back. "And you, Josephus, you'd better not cause
complaints by your wild conduct."

"But in gym and singing we both have very good," Joey
said. "And it's a very good report card, isn't it, Mummy?"

"Very good," Mother said, taking each of the boys in one
arm. "Maybe it will be still better at Easter time. Yes, they're
amazing report cards and I'm proud of you both, and of you,
Andrea."

Mrs. Verduz sat in one corner of the sofa and Margret in
the other, the big cat purring contentedly between them.
Margret was so absorbed in the book from Mrs. Verduz that
she did not see or hear what was going on around her. It was
the *Odyssey*. The evening passed so quickly that nobody
knew what had become of it. When Mother said, "Now we
must put on our coats and go out for Christmas Mass," none
of them could believe it was already so late.

Through the crisp cold of the silent streets they went to
the small chapel in the Ursuline Convent where the mass
was to be celebrated. There, under the glittering tree, stood
the crêche with its many wisps of straw, each contributed
by some little girl who had done a good deed. And the
Christ Child on the straw looked alive. Who was it that
kneeled behind the manger and looked down upon the
Child with such deep devotion? None other than Andrea
with a blue mantle over her red dress and her long dark hair
falling around her shoulders. Joseph with a beard of cotton-

wool stood behind her, two angels at either side, and shepherds in shaggy sheepskins knelt and prayed at her feet.

The incense floated up in little clouds, the candles shone and the bells of the acolytes tinkled. Everywhere in the churches of the city the homeless exiles knelt and prayed side by side with the natives, and to them all the consoling voice of the angel sang, "Fear not."

On the way home the children were very still. They were filled with all the events of the day; they were so tired they could scarcely keep their eyes open, and their hearts were full and warm with the joy of Christmas.

"I have not had such a lovely Christmas for many years," Mrs. Verduz said as they bade each other good night on the stairs.

The two younger boys were to sleep together. Matthias had borrowed an old mattress from Mrs. Verduz and was camping in his mother's room for the holidays. Mother tucked the two little boys in snug, and the big girls as well, and gave each of them a good night kiss.

"It was swell," Hans Ulrich sighed from the bottom of his heart.

In the sisters' bed Margret said to Andrea, "Why don't you let me sleep against the wall tonight, even though it is your turn. After all, it's Christmas."

"It's Christmas for me, too," Andrea said.

When Matthias was already asleep on his mattress, Mother lit a candle and read Margret's poem:

> *Far, far away*
> *Is the home we love*
> *But the selfsame stars*
> *Look down from above.*

And one of the stars
Which shines so bright
Leads the good shepherds
To the Child of Light.

Oh Child in the manger
Whom Mary covers now,
We too are strangers
And as poor as Thou.

Upon those who have died
Thy peace bestow
And cover their graves
With the soft white snow.

From prison and camp
Let Father go free,
And bring him back safe
Over mountain and sea.

The candlelight moved across the hallway into the cold bedroom. It hovered for a moment above the sleeping boys and above Andrea, whose black pigtails alone showed above the blankets, and was reflected in Margret's wide-awake eyes.

"Thank you, Margret," Mother said, and her face bent down to Margret's. "God bless you."

Two days after Christmas Matthias and Dieter tramped out to Rowan Farm, pulling the little cart behind them. It was a frosty but beautiful day. After noon the sun actually came out for a short while. They pitched right into the work.

Mrs. Almut herself came out to where they were chopping, brought them lunch and praised them for doing such clean and fast work.

"It's a pity you didn't bring your sister with you," she said. "How do you figure on getting your wood back to town?"

"My friend will come out with his truck tomorrow," Dieter answered for Matthias, "and they'll have it loaded up in no time."

"Well, you're pretty well off, having a friend with a truck," Mrs. Almut said. "You're good workers, you two. I wish I had a sturdy young fellow to work for me. Old Joseph won't be able to handle things alone when the spring work starts, and my son is still in a prisoner-of-war camp. Even if he were here we'd hardly get through; there's so much to do in the orchard and with the tree nursery as soon as we have the weather for it. But I suppose you have too many other interests to care about farming and gardening."

"A while back I wanted to study gardening," Matthias said. "But I couldn't find a place anywhere as an apprentice."

"An apprentice, eh," the pony woman said. "Funny, I never thought of that. But why shouldn't I take an apprentice? I studied nursery gardening with Blumenschmidt in Erfurt years and years ago and rate as a master gardener myself. There's certainly plenty you could learn around here. Only it's no eight-hour-a-day job; an apprentice who worked for me would have to lend a hand in the stables and in the fields. That's the only way we can manage. How old are you, anyway?"

"I'll be sixteen in March," Matthias said, his head reeling. He could scarcely believe in such a lucky break for him.

"Sixteen. Well. And you're big and strong, too. You're thin for your size, but we would attend to that here. The question is, would you like it? I'd want you to understand that the job means a great deal of work and not much pay. What do you think?" she asked, turning to Dieter.

"I don't think you could find anyone better," Dieter said firmly.

"Well, think it over," Mrs. Almut said. "Right after New Year's I'm coming to town to pick up dog meat. I'll drop in on your folks then."

Toward evening, after they had piled Mrs. Almut's wood and their own in separate heaps, they loaded their cart with trimmed-out brush and trudged along with it down the hill toward the town.

"Well, how does life strike you now?" Dieter asked after they had walked in silence for a long time, each busy with his own thoughts.

"Do you think she'll take me?"

"Of course she will."

"But you didn't think I was suitable material for your band."

"Good Lord, Matthias, has that been on your mind? I never even considered it—I knew that wouldn't be the right life for you. You want to learn a real trade, and that's what you'll be able to do out at the farm there. You don't want to turn into a gypsy like me."

Tired and heavy-footed, the two friends entered the warm attic room in Parsley Street.

"Sit down on the sofa, woodchoppers," Margret said. "I'll make you some blackberry tea right away."

Andrea was reading. She kept her hands cupped over her

ears so she could concentrate better. She was reading the book Mrs. Verduz had given her for Christmas: *Shakespeare's Plays*.

"It looks like Matthias is going to be getting a job," Dieter announced after a while, nudging Matthias encouragingly.

"What!" everyone cried at once, and even Andrea took her hands away from her ears.

"At Mrs. Almut's," Matthias said. "The pony woman. She wants to come and discuss it with you right after New Year's, Mummy."

"The pony woman!" Margret burst out, and she fell into a chair. "And there you sit looking so calm. Matthias, Matthias! Some people have all the luck."

CHAPTER SEVEN

Mrs. Almut Comes

HANS ULRICH stayed at their house all through the Christmas holidays. He and Joey wanted to be read *The Treasure in the Cellar* every night. The book was short enough to be finished in three or four evenings, but the trouble was that as soon as it was read through it had to be started all over again. And one or the other of the girls had to read it. Soon they were bored to death with it. But Hans Ulrich and Joey pleaded so sweetly and were so faithful about drying the supper dishes that it was hard to resist them—although Andrea and Margret would much rather have read their own books. Matthias usually sat at a corner of the table and read an outmoded but fascinating little book on astronomy which had turned up among the possessions of Mrs. Verduz's sainted husband. The whole family agreed that it was fortunate that there were still some people who were not refugees and hadn't been bombed out, people who still had houses filled with useful things and forgotten books accumulated by generations.

No one guessed what a tremendous influence *The Treasure in the Cellar* was having upon the minds of Hans Ulrich and Joey. If they had guessed, the sisters would never have begun the book. But the story had become an obsession with the boys. It was about someone who found a chest full of precious gold and silver coins that had been buried in a cellar by a miser many years ago. Why in the world shouldn't something of the same sort happen nowadays. After all, there were plenty of rubble-filled cellars where treasures might be hidden. If anyone could find a treasure, they could. And so the two boys used the scant daylight of the short winter days to look for hidden treasure in "their" ruin near the schoolhouse. At home they generously promised presents to all members of the family—since they were certain to be rich before long. They spared no pains and certainly did not spare their clothing, but in spite of a week's digging they brought home nothing but holes in their stockings and tears in their pants.

All this made more work for Margret. One evening during Christmas week Margret was sitting with the overflowing darning basket beside her. As usual, Caliph crouched in her lap. This was his established right. If Margret were doing anything at which a cat could help, Caliph was there.

After a while Mother said, "Someone told me of a seamstress who will probably take an apprentice around April first. I think we ought to go around to see her tomorrow. If we don't get you placed right away, the Labor Office will be sending you off to a factory."

"But I'm not very good at sewing," Margret said.

"What else would you like to learn?"

"I don't know. If only Mrs. Almut would take me."

"I hope she'll take Matthias. And I think the work would be too hard for you anyhow. You'll see, once you get the hang of sewing you'll like it."

"Possibly," Margret said. She did not want to be stubborn and she had long ago realized that you couldn't do whatever you wanted.

"You'll be seventeen when you finish your apprenticeship," Mother said. "Then the two of us will easily be able to make enough for ourselves and the two younger ones. Matthias is already standing on his own feet, and perhaps times will improve. Come, don't look so sad; there are lots worse things in the world than learning to sew."

Margret could no longer keep back her tears; the whole subject somehow made her feel terrible. "It doesn't matter one way or the other," she sobbed. "Life will never be good again anyway."

"That's the sort of thing you think when you're young," Mother said.

Margret stopped crying. She did not want to break down that way. But becoming a seamstress did not interest her; it was simply not what she wanted to do. What wonderful luck Matthias had. When she thought of him she found it hard not to feel envy. Not that she didn't wish him all the happiness in the world, but here he was, having this wonderful job offered him, and he didn't even seem to realize just how lucky he was. It was plain waste for him to be so lucky when he didn't even appreciate it.

When January second arrived the whole family waited in great suspense. One or the other of the children kept running to the window. But Mrs. Almut did not come.

"She must have changed her mind," Matthias said, and

although he had not shown his anticipation, he now looked terribly disappointed. The construction job had begun again, and it was dreary without Dieter. Three times a week Matthias was still meeting Dieter at the café for their violin and piano duets, but that was pretty small potatoes for Dieter now. Dieter was up to his ears in work, rehearsing his little band. He already had a lot of engagements. Soon Dieter wouldn't be interested in the café job, Matthias thought, and he saw his own future as lonely and bleak. January second was a bad day for Matthias.

But on January third horses' hoofs were heard clattering down Parsley Street. Margret rushed to the window. "There she is," she shouted, and went clumping down the stairs without for a moment thinking of poor Mrs. Verduz's nerves. She pulled open the front door. There stood the steaming ponies in front of their old cart, and the little woman with the fur cap clambered down from the box and gave Margret a friendly smile. "Good day," she said. "Is your mother home?"

Margret nodded. She was so happy and relieved that she could not say a word. Only now did she realize how much she had really wanted Matthias to get the job at Mrs. Almut's.

"Would you mind holding the ponies?" Mrs. Almut said.

Would she mind! Margret clambered up on the box and took the reins. Some of the children playing in the street gathered around the cart and stared at her respectfully. It was good to have the feel of reins in her hands once more, and it was good, too, to be admired for a change. That was something that didn't often happen to a refugee child.

How the backs of the horses shone. Oh, it would be good

to sit astride a horse once more and ride across a field. The two ponies stood rather restlessly; it was quite clear that they were sick of the city and wanted to go home. They tossed their heads, shaking their fine silken manes from side to side; they stamped with their little hoofs and shook their harness. Feeling sorry for them, Margret got down and stood by their heads. She did not even notice that she had forgotten to put on her coat and that her feet were gradually turning to lumps of ice. The ponies sniffed cautiously at her. She stood very still until she felt a delicate, soft muzzle against her face, and her heart pounded for sheer happiness. Suddenly the wet muzzle moved away. Something had frightened the horse. She tossed her head high, twitched her ears and rolled her dark eyes wildly. But only for a moment. Then her muzzle pressed again into Margret's caressing hand. Margret leaned her cheek against the silky smoothness of the pony's neck and breathed in the good horsy smell. She spoke to the horses in the gentle, quiet voice that animals like. She did not know how long she stood there. Suddenly the pony woman reappeared. "Well, made friends already?" she said. "Go up and get your coat—you can ride a little way with me."

Margret was up and down in a moment. "I'll be right back," she called to her mother as she shot down the stairs. She climbed up to the box beside Mrs. Almut. The ponies were already champing to go. "Can you drive?" Mrs. Almut asked. She handed the reins to Margret and the ponies dashed off. They took the corner a little roughly, but missed the curb, and both Margret and Mrs. Almut laughed like two happy children. Margret could have burst out singing just for the joy of handling the horses.

"Can you milk?" Mrs. Almut asked abruptly.

Margret shook her head sadly. Of course that was another thing that stood against her. What good was someone who couldn't milk on a farm?

"I'd like to learn to milk if I got the chance," she said. "At home in Pomerania milking wasn't considered dainty work. On good farms not even the servant girls would milk; that would be in the agreement before the mothers would let the girls go out to work. For milking they always had an old woman come in from the village."

"We're not so dainty here," Mrs. Almut said. "I can milk and do it myself every morning."

"I always thought it must be fun to milk. It's just that they never let me learn. Is Matthias really going to work for you?"

"I'm on my way to the Labor Office now to see about it. I know the people there. They'll release him from the construction job for farm work—you just have to know how to talk to them. The only question is whether they'll let me take him on as an apprentice. And what are you planning to do?"

"Learn to be a seamstress." Margret's tone made no secret of the way she felt.

"Is that already settled?"

"Not yet. But it will be soon. What else can I do? Everything I'd like to do I can't."

"Do you really think you'd like to clean dog kennels, curry four dogs every day, take them for runs, feed them, get up at six o'clock and milk, do housework and help Kathrin in the kitchen? And get very, very little pay for all that?"

Margret stared unbelievingly at her. Mrs. Almut was smil-

ing so broadly that she looked like a jolly little gnome underneath the round fur hat.

"Are you asking that just . . . just for fun?" Margret
asked tonelessly. It was awful; she was all choked up.

"You have to talk louder with all this noise. Would you
care to?"

"Care to?" Margret shouted, and she hurriedly swallowed
the lump in her throat and gave the reins such a jerk that
the ponies almost turned the cart over. "Care to? I couldn't
think of anything more wonderful."

"Well—you'd better think it over. I warn you, it's hard
work. You'll ache in every bone of your body."

"I don't care, I don't care," Margret cried happily. "Just
tell me you really mean it."

"Well, I'd like to try you. I want Matthias as soon as possible. There's time enough for you until March first. In March
Ate is expecting her new litter of pups and the sheep will be
lambing; then our work really begins. I've already talked it
over with your mother."

They stopped in front of the Labor Office. Mrs. Almut got
out and Margret stayed with the ponies again. It was a long
while before Mrs. Almut reappeared. Her fur cap was all
askew on her head; she looked almost as if she had been
through a fight in the boxing ring, but there was no doubt
that she had won. "Those numbskulls, those bureaucrats,"
she said. "Ha. But I gave them what for. 'Don't come to us
about it,' they said, 'it's not our affair.' The people to see
were the Agricultural Department or the Grange. I'm not
taking that kind of run-around. I didn't let them get away
with that."

"Will you get permission for Matthias and me to move?"

Margret asked worriedly. She felt that if anything came up to interfere now, she simply would not be able to bear it.

But Mrs. Almut nodded confidently. "It's all one district, after all, and it's easier to get people from city to country than the other way round. I have room for you, too—that is, we'll make room. Though it won't be very comfortable at first. The mayor of our little village knows that I supply more produce than most of the other farmers, and he'll do me a favor if he can. Now run along home, Margret, and talk everything over with your mother. When I come for Matthias, you can give me your answer. But think it over carefully. Once I've trained you, I won't want you running off on me just when the main work starts in the spring."

"Good-by," Margret called radiantly. "Till next time!" She patted the ponies' necks. "I'm coming to live with you," she whispered into their twitching ears. Then she ran toward Parsley Street as fast as she could.

It took almost three weeks before all the complications with the Labor Office were straightened out and Mrs. Almut was finally able to bring Matthias out to Rowan Farm. His mother was glad that he would be leaving the construction work which he had never liked for the wholesome life in the country. She was glad, too, that he would be working for Mrs. Almut; the two women had liked each other at once. But Mother was still a little worried. Did Matthias really have strength enough for all the hard work he would be asked to do, after the lean years behind him? And might there not be so much farm and field work that he would not get much gardening training? And finally, Matthias was the sort of boy who should be working with his mind as well as with his hands. Was it good to let him bury himself in the country where there was no chance for him to further his education? And now Margret would be leaving too. Mrs. Lechow felt heartsick when she thought of losing her two big children at once, but she could not be so cruel as to say no. Margret herself was happy and absolutely certain that her life was at last taking the turn she wanted. No amount of describing how hard the work would be would make her reconsider. The only thing that clouded her joy was the thought that her mother might have a difficult time without her.

The person who made the most fuss about the children's leaving was Mrs. Verduz. Who would chop her wood now and help with the housework? Why it was just terrible to have the two oldest leaving; it was a real tragedy for an old woman like herself who could no longer do all her own work. Mrs. Verduz sat hunched up on her chair in the kitchen, in a state of utter despair, and told Andrea that she would never survive it if she had to overtax herself now.

"But I'll still be here," Andrea said, feeling sorry for her. "You'll see, Mrs. Verduz, when Lenchen and I get finished with our homework the two of us will come down and clean house for you and wash the dishes and everything. I'm going to be doing the shopping for Mother on the way to school anyhow. Around noon the stores aren't so full and I'll just pick up your things at the same time. Joey and Hans Ulrich can carry up your wood. It will be good for them to have some chores; then they won't have so much time for that silly treasure digging. And old Mr. Lebenow can chop wood for you. He's still plenty strong enough, though he won't do it as fast as Matthias, of course. . . . And don't you see, now there'll be only three of us which is just one more than the childless couple you wanted right along."

But even this last consideration did not console Mrs. Verduz. It took a while before Andrea's persuasiveness revived her spirits.

On January twenty-second the hoofs of the ponies once more clattered down Parsley Street. People stared curiously from all the windows as Margret came down to hold the ponies and the woman in the fur cap went into the house and after a while reappeared with Matthias. Matthias threw his rucksack into the cart, clambered up on the box, shook hands with his sister once more and waved up at the gable window where his mother was looking down. It felt odd to be leaving. Then the ponies started off, and Margret remained behind, standing alone on the cobblestones of Parsley Street and thinking, half with longing and half with sadness: Soon I'll be going too.

At least they had been all together to celebrate Joey's seventh birthday in the middle of January, when the cold was at its bitterest. Joey's best birthday present came from school—the schools stayed closed through most of January because of the coal shortage. But Mother had insisted that he spend a full hour every morning sitting beside her sewing machine and working with his book and slate. Even in adversity Hans Ulrich stuck by him, and that was some consolation. But how mean letters and numbers could be! They seemed made on purpose to make life difficult for the two boys and to steal the time they could be using for more important work. And having Margret for a teacher was even worse than having Mummy, who at least was patient. On the other hand, Margret was good at inventing ways to make lessons a little more interesting.

They would want to be reading their own books soon, Margret pointed out, and all the others in the big chest in the other room. Besides which, what good would the richest treasure do them if they did not know enough arithmetic to divide it up. "Suppose," she said, "you found a chest with ten gold pieces and ten silver pieces. How much would each of you get?"

"That wouldn't be enough," Hans Ulrich said. "A big chest would have to have more."

"Well, figure this out first."

With frowning faces, they sat and pondered the problem. At last Joey had an inspiration. "I'll take the gold pieces," he proposed, "and Hans Ulrich can have the silver."

"But I want the gold," Hans Ulrich objected. "Gold is worth more than silver and I'm poorer than you."

In a moment they were bickering like cat and dog. Margret took each of the treasure hunters by the collar and put them back in their chairs. "You see," she said. "You have to learn arithmetic or you'll half kill each other. How much is half of ten?"

"Oh well, if you'd only said that right off. You got us all mixed up with your gold and silver pieces."

It was a sore trial for them, but by the end of January their store of knowledge had obviously increased. With a good deal of stammering, groaning and sounding out they could manage to make out simple reading material, and they were even beginning to think it fun. In arithmetic they would have been able to handle a treasure amounting to the dizzying sum of thirty gold and thirty silver pieces.

During those terribly cold weeks Margret hated more than ever the hours of standing in line in front of stores. Her feet would gradually turn numb, her hands itched and prickled with chilblains, and finally the cold would go so deeply into her that she wanted to cry. How lucky it was, she often thought, that she was still home and Mother did not have to go through this miserable waiting in line. By the time she left in March spring would be near, and then nothing would be so bad.

When Mrs. Almut and Matthias reached Rowan Farm, she showed him right away how to unhitch the ponies and stable and feed them. Then they went into the house to have a cup of hot milk and thick slices of bread spread with syrup, for they were cold from riding in the open cart. Afterwards, Mrs. Almut showed her new apprentice around the farmyard so that he would know what was what. Opposite the house was the cowbarn; next to that the pigsty and the dogs' kitchen, then the laundry and the wagon and machine shed, and finally the horse stable which opened out into a large corral. The two ponies had the main stable to themselves; the stallion Lumpi had his own stable and run on the other side of the yard. Above the stables was plenty of storage space for hay and grain, and there was also another large haybarn on the other side of the yard, adjoining the kennels. The east side of the farmyard was closed in by an odd-looking building. On second glance this turned out to be an old railroad car that had been set up on a high foundation of stone—the space underneath it was used to store cordwood and all sorts of tools.

"That's been here for ten years now," Mrs. Almut said. "Those were the days when the railroad company used to sell its old cars for a song. I thought I was going to use it for a large kennel. But I never got around to making it over, and of latter years I've thought it would make a nice house for my old age, when Bernd comes back and maybe marries. But that's a while away; right now it's your palace, although you'll have some work to do to make it comfortable."

Following her, Matthias climbed up the steps of the car. The inside was in fairly good shape. In fact, compared with the cars currently being used on the German railroads it was practically luxurious.

"First thing you ought to do is to fix up one of the seats as a bed. If you nailed a board in front, the mattress wouldn't slide down. Later on you might take out some of the compartment partitions. There's room, I figure, for two little bedrooms and a fairly good-sized kitchen-living room. You'll have a chance to work on it quite a lot before the spring chores start. By the time your sister comes I think you can make it fairly nice. What do you say?"

"Oh, I'll fix it up fine," Matthias said. "A villa all for ourselves. Won't Margret be surprised."

"All right, then. I'll give you blankets and a featherbed. You'll find a sack for a straw mattress in the barn. Don't stuff it too tight or it will be hard."

"Don't worry, I'm an expert on straw mattresses from living in camps."

"The washbasin in the toilet is still in perfect order. All you have to do is clean everything up nicely. When Margret moves in here in March she'll be near the sheep so she can keep an eye on them. You see, right here at the back you look out on the big sheep run with the pines and the elderberry bushes. The shed over there is the sheep barn."

She tripped down the steps, calling out, "You'll have to build yourself a veranda in the summer," and ran across the yard toward the house. She was like a weasel, always moving, always on the jump. In spite of her sixty-one years she looked like a young girl, slim and limber, as she sped across the yard.

Mrs. Almut was not the only resident on the farm. Sharing her house was the white-haired professor who had greeted the children so cordially when they came carol-singing. He lived on the ground floor in a room opposite Mrs. Almut's. His wife had been Mrs. Almut's closest girlhood friend. The professor's home in Frankfurt had been destroyed in the bombings and he had only a few of his old possessions left, chief among them his books and a few priceless things he had brought from China which he had earlier taken to the safety of Rowan Farm.

Kathrin's room was on the top floor. Years ago Kathrin had been Mrs. Almut's housekeeper. Then she had married and moved away to Silesia. Her husband and son had fallen on the Russian front; she had been driven from house and home and now, weary and sick, she had returned to Mrs. Almut and been received with kindness. She was not much older than Mrs. Almut herself, but she looked old enough to be her mother and could no longer do much work. Stooped old Joseph who lived in another little room on the top floor was also handicapped by age. But he kept busy from morning to night and would say again and again that he had to keep going at least until Bernd returned.

There was also a tiny room where Ling, the professor's Chinese servant, lived. The farmhouse was really full up—

but Matthias counted himself lucky having a whole building to himself.

Matthias stood looking around his mansion, and with the lively imagination of all the Lechow children he saw the old railroad car already transformed into a sturdy cottage, completely furnished, with a little lane of birch trees leading up to the door and a little garden with a fence around it to keep out the sheep. He would have loved to start carpentering at once. But while he stood lost in dreams, Joseph's voice came across the yard. "Get on your workclothes and come over to the stable; it's time for feeding."

Quickly, he put on his old ski pants and his heavy grey sweater and hurried across to the stable. There Joseph showed him how much hay the ponies got at night, and how much hay went to the cows. Every evening the manure had to be carted away and fresh straw spread, so that the animals could bed down clean and warm. Next Joseph took him to the sheep, who in this icy weather could no longer find feed out of doors. "Your sister will take these over later," Joseph said. "We'll appreciate that when our spring work begins. And now that scamp Lumpi has to be looked to. He's a wicked beast. Come along."

The wicked beast stood in his small stable beside the woodshed. He laid his ears flat when the men entered. It was perfectly clear that he and Joseph did not get along. According to Joseph, the stallion was a kicker and a biter. "He has a mean nature," Joseph said. "The only one who can do anything with him is Mrs. Almut."

The horse was like a wild creature, sensitive, shy and nervous, but so beautiful that Matthias had to exclaim. He was golden brown, with the head of a miniature Arabian

stallion, and large, dark, brightly moist eyes. Matthias spoke
softly to him as he put down the oats. But Lumpi did not
want to be made friends with. He shook his mane and stood
alert, ready to kick out if anyone came too close. Luckily,
he was not yet shod.

They went through Lumpi's run and past the henhouse
to the orchard, where the berry bushes leaned against their
wire supports. Nearby were the long rows of young trees in
the nursery garden, the strawberry field, the raspberries and
the blackberries.

"There'll be a lot of winter-kill this year," Joseph said. "It's
been so cold, and before the cold weather almost all the
good snow we had around Christmas melted away. I can't
remember a winter as bad as this. The winter wheat is done
for already; we'll have to plow it over as soon as the weather
opens up. And tomorrow we must start carting out the
manure."

Carting manure was certainly not a glorious way to begin
life on Rowan Farm. The stuff did not smell good, and Matthias himself did not smell good when he came back from
the fields. But there were no two ways about it, the manure
had to be spread. Worse than the smell was the way his every
muscle ached. He felt as if his arms were about to fall off
from lifting and scattering hundreds of heavily-laden fork-
fuls of manure.

"Take it easy, boy," Joseph said. "There's a knack to everything." Joseph was not a hard taskmaster, but the work had
to be done; it had its own laws. Nothing could be put off on
the farm.

Rowan Farm was not a large place. It had only about fifty
tillable acres. In addition to this there was some woodland

and a stretch of moor where the sheep grazed in summer. It was hard work to make a living out of the place, for the soil here at the foot of the mountains was far from rich. Matthias learned something about the history of the farm from Joseph. The Almuts had bought it shortly after the First World War, when they decided to get out of the city. Mrs. Almut had worked in the nursery of a large seed company and her husband had been a painter. Neither of them had known too much about farming when they started out, but they had been hard-working and intelligent, and sensitive to the ways of nature, of soil and woods, plants and animals.

Little good fortune came their way. Mr. Almut was killed in an accident when his son was only two, and his wife had to face the hard struggles of the early years alone. She bore up bravely and went on farming. She took up dog-breeding and was successful at it. After years of conscientious breeding the fame of her kennel spread through Germany and abroad. Her dogs were much in demand by American breeders and brought high prices. In this way she was able to pay off her most pressing debts.

Her son Bernd followed in his mother's steps and went to work for the seed company as an apprentice. When he came back, he started to build up a nursery and orchard at home. The farm began really to prosper. But the war destroyed all their hopes. In 1942, when Bernd had to leave for the army, prospects looked dark indeed. But Mrs. Almut had not let the difficulties get her down. Through all sorts of cares and trials she had managed to hold her head above water and keep up the farm so that it would be there for her son when he returned.

Matthias used every spare minute to fix up his house.
Everyone contributed something. Kathrin gave him two
chairs, Joseph gave him a wobbly table, and Mrs. Almut
hunted up an old rug. It was lucky he had done so much
work with hammer, nails and saw during the past few
months. All that skill came in handy now. For the time being he fixed up a single compartment as a temporary bedroom for himself. But by the time Margret came the place
would have to look a bit different. In the woodshed he found
an ancient iron stove that proved to be still usable.

"Take it," Mrs. Almut said when he asked her about it.
"But you'll have to get your own wood from the woodlot.
Our own supply will hardly last us through because it's been
such a hard winter."

All very well—if only the days had been longer! But no
matter how he tried to arrange things, every day was a few
hours too short. On his first Sunday he would have liked to
walk to town, for he wanted very much to see his mother,
and even his sisters and Joey seemed at this distance the most
lovable people in the world. When they were together they
often squabbled, but they still clung to each other. But no, he
couldn't take the time for a visit. There was too much to do
on his day off. Right after the morning's barn work he
pitched into "construction." The winter sun shone with
amazing warmth, and that was good because his hands didn't
freeze while working. Before long Matthias took off his
jacket and worked in his shirtsleeves. His blond forelock
hung down over his forehead and his light skin began red-
dening. In spite of tiredness and aching muscles, he felt
wonderfully strong and alive.

As he worked a number of visitors dropped in to encourage

him. Mrs. Almut stood around for a quarter of an hour and praised his skill. She had brought Lumpi with her into the sheepfold; he ran along behind her like a dog, rubbing his muzzle against her cheek as she stood and talked with Matthias. The horse watched Matthias intently, and seemed almost disposed to be friendly. But when Matthias made a move to stroke him, Lumpi shied away.

When Matthias went out again right after dinner, the professor came with him to see how much progress had been made. On Sundays the professor always ate with the rest of them; during the week Ling prepared his meals separately and served them in fragile bowls of Chinese porcelain.

It was as though everybody wanted to say a friendly word to the youngest member of Rowan Farm.

The old professor looked on for a while, asked a few questions, and before he knew how he got onto the subject, Matthias had confessed that his real dream had been to be an astronomer.

"Gardening fits in beautifully with that," the professor said.

Matthias stopped hammering for a moment and looked up in amazement. He asked the professor what he meant. The fact was, he said, he had given up all hope of studying; there was no use thinking about it.

"You don't have to go to a university to study astronomy," the old gentleman said. "There have been a good many astronomers whose regular profession was something quite different. For example Pastor Dörffel, who had one of the mountains of the moon named after him, and the farmer astronomers Ludewig and Arnold. If there is something you

love, you must not give it up, even though there may seem
little prospect of your doing anything with it."

"But you'd need to have books and a telescope," Matthias
said.

"All my life I have believed that everything you really
need and deserve will come in its time. The ancient Chinese
say that you must learn to know reality in order to be wise.
Well, there is reality enough for you here. Whether you look
at a blade of grass or the stars in the sky, one is as wonderful
as the other, and what you discover in the grass will teach
you how better to understand the stars."

"I will think about that," Matthias said. "I'd about decided
that I would have to put all that out of my mind, because it
would only make me sad. But maybe that was stupid of me.
You've given me a very different way to look at everything."

The second Sunday Matthias did walk to the city, although it was cold and snowing on and off. He had been
away from home only two weeks, but it seemed to him that
he was received like a rare and honored guest. At first his
sisters and brother were speechless with respect—which was
a very pleasant reception for a young man who had worked
like a horse all week. When his mother asked him about
everything, he answered tersely and to the point, sounding
just like an old and experienced farmer. He did not mention
that his back ached every night or that his feet were sore
from his clumsy shoes. But he did tell the family that he was
already in sole charge of the ponies and that both of them
would lift their heads and whinny when he came in.

After the family's awe had somewhat subsided, they all
began talking at once. Mother scarcely had a chance to ask

the questions she had saved up—who was doing his laundry and whether the work really was not too strenuous for him and whether he had enough covers at night. Margret pelted him with questions about the animals, especially the dogs, and was delighted to hear about the stallion Lumpi who would tolerate only women.

At last the honored guest turned to his younger brother, who was hopping around on one foot in his eagerness to get a word in. "What have you got to say, squirt?"

The story burst out of Joey like a pent-up torrent. "You know what, Mat, we're going to find the treasure sure as anything. We've dug through to a door already and believe me it was hard work and . . ."

"Anyone could tell that from the condition of your stockings," Margret interrupted.

"Be quiet, it isn't your turn now. The door looks just like Open Sesame, you know, Ali Baba's, and you wait and see what we find once we get it open. All we need now is an ax."

"Have mercy on us," Mother moaned. "Next thing you know you'll be chopping your fingers off."

Later, Matthias went to visit Dieter in his cellar apartment. On the door hung a brightly-painted sign: The Cellar Rats. Music for all Occasions. Rhythmic sounds greeted Matthias as he entered. The Cellar Rats were practicing. There was actually a piano in the cellar, somewhat scratched and scarred, but obviously in order and perfectly in tune. The band also had two violins, a saxophone, a drum and cymbals, and two guitars and a mandolin. Some of the instruments Hans and Dieter had brought back from their expedition into the Russian zone, some of them had been donated by the youth warden and the pastor's wife. But more amazing than the instruments was the way the boys could handle all of them alternately. Dieter was a stern conductor; he allowed no sloppiness either in singing or playing. When someone failed to come in like a pistol shot, precisely on time, or when an instrument or voice was just the slightest bit off key, he would roar like a lion and rage like a madman—Dieter who ordinarily was the soul of calm.

As soon as the greetings were over, they insisted on having Matthias hear the new Cellar Rat song Dieter had composed, and for which one of the other boys had written the words. For a few bars a flute twittered shyly like the first bird in springtime. Violin, saxophone and guitar came in, a fine baritone voice began singing, and four others joined it. What was it all about, this song of theirs? It was a song of the highway, a song of returning prisoners, of the long tramp through the dust of summer highways and through winter snows, of shattered walls where once a home had stood, of the laughter of girls and the bitterness of a lonely man, the dead mother and the lost sweetheart—but above it all the little trills of the bird rang out cheerfully and impudently into the cold, merciless winter world. The bird insisted on its belief that spring would soon be coming again.

Matthias said nothing when the song was over. When something moved him deeply, he could not speak of it; that was just the way he was. But Dieter understood anyhow.

"Gee, but you're fancy," Matthias said at last, to fill in the awkward pause. With astonishment he inspected the neat brown shirts and trousers the musicians were wearing.

"From the Amis," they told him smugly. "We've been twice to play in the American bar, and now it's going to be a regular thing. They gave us shirts and pants so we wouldn't look so ragged."

"There's a captain there who's our patron," Dieter explained. "He asked us to play in a soldier's club and has done a lot of other things to help us."

Later, when Dieter was alone with Matthias, he said, "It's beginning to mean something, don't you think? If I were off studying, the boys would be out on the streets busy with Black Market deals and sitting up nights over drinks and cigarettes and cards. I'm glad things have turned out this way. We'll wait and see what happens next."

"I don't suppose you could squeeze in any time for me, could you?" Matthias asked cautiously.

"Of course I have time for you. Do you need a hand with something?"

"Could you come out some Sunday and help me work on my house?"

"Your house? You've come a long way pretty fast. Our engagements are in the evening. I'll come out first thing on a Sunday morning. All right? So long."

CHAPTER EIGHT

Young People and Young Animals

THE FIRST of March was a Saturday, a bright and almost springlike day with white clouds sweeping across a light blue sky, with lanes of melting snow between the dark brown plow furrows and lavender veils among the swaying branches of the birches. On the trees along the road to Hellborn a few solitary male blackbirds sat practicing their courting songs.

The children had decided that they would all accompany Margret to Rowan Farm. They set out right after noon. Mrs. Almut had invited all of them, including Lenchen and Hans Ulrich, to share in the big pot of pea soup that was made at Rowan Farm for Saturday afternoons. After all, it was time Mother took a good look at the place that was now home for two of her brood.

At the Big Tower Margret turned around once more to look back at the city. It lay grey and misty in the lowlands, while up here the sun shone brightly and to the east the great wave of the mountains rose, alluring and menacing at one

and the same time. It was a day for hiking; the sunny line
of the highway literally drew you along into the bright
distances. The brooks rushed and leaped, the clouds floated
quietly along, and beneath them flew dark flocks of birds.
How glad Margret would have been to be leaving the city
behind her, if only it weren't so hard to be deserting her
mother. Now, at the last minute, she felt that she ought not
to be running off into a new and wonderful life while
Mother remained behind with her sewing machine and all
her household worries in the cramped quarters on Parsley
Street.

"Are you happy, Margret?" Mother asked as though guess-
ing her thoughts. Margret gave her mother a look of utter
despair. She was happy, terribly happy, but her happiness
hurt her and she felt almost ashamed of it.

"Yes, I'm happy. I'm awfully selfish, though, Mummy. I
wish I knew how all of you are going to make out alone."

"Why, there are only three of us now. That's a small
enough household. Oh yes, Hans Ulrich, I know you belong
to us too. So let's say three and a half. And I really think
that sitting home at the machine all the time isn't good for
me. I always used to be on the move; I'm not used to sitting
still. It will do me good to start running around again some.
But I'll get a lot of sewing in, too."

"And then I'm still there," Andrea said. "I'll do the shopping on the way to school. And at night I'll peel the potatoes,
trala, and spring is coming, and in the morning before school
I'll sweep the steps, tralala, and Mrs. Verduz's kitchen, and
Saturdays I'll do the scouring." She was clasping Lenchen's
hand, and whenever she took a hop, skip and jump, fat little
Lenchen had to hop with her.

"If you come to our store, you won't have to stand in line at all, Mrs. Lechow," Lenchen said; she was as eager as the others to be helpful. "On Fridays all you have to do is give me a note saying what you want, and the ration stamps too, and I'll bring you your order."

Hans Ulrich's face glowed with sudden inspiration. "And I'll have my foster mother do the mending for me again. Once we get the treasure I can pay her for it. And when I come to dinner with you I'll help dry the dishes."

"You're good at that," Andrea agreed. "Usually you lick the plate so clean we don't even have to wash it."

"And I'll bring up the wood," Joey said. "I could bring some two-by-fours from our ruin, too."

"You see, Margret," Mother said. "With such helpful children I'll have nothing to do but sit around all day long and twiddle my thumbs."

At the corner of Rowan Road, where it turned off from the highway and led up to the farm—the words *Rowan Farm* were cut into the stone bench that stood there—Matthias stood waiting for them. He had Fury with him. In the kennel Alf and Arjopa, the young hounds, were yapping. Ate, their mother, lay stretched out in the sun, barking occasionally to keep them company.

Mrs. Almut greeted them in the hall, and almost immediately Kathrin carried in the huge tureen filled with pea soup. Margret shook hands with the cook. She was a little afraid of the brusque old woman. But Kathrin looked quite friendly today.

"And now," Matthias said when they were finished eating, "I'll show you where we live."

Margret would have preferred visiting the animals first.

But Matthias headed straight for the railroad car, climbed the steps and opened the door with an expansive gesture. "Here?" the family exclaimed in amazement. "But it's a railroad car." The girls rushed up the steps, but the two little boys first had to examine the underpinning carefully. "It's got a cellar," they shouted from under the car. "But all the wheels are gone. Too bad."

Margret was holding her mother's hand. She drew her from the corridor into the bedroom which Matthias had made into a real little room by taking out a partition. "Look at this, Mummy," she cried. "A room with two beds and a table and chair and even a stove. There's a fire in it right now."

Matthias led them all around like the caretaker of a famous palace, and his visitors were as impressed as any group of sight-seers. They liked the beds best of all, although these were nothing but hard third-class benches rimmed with a board and filled with a straw mattress. But the beds looked so comfortable with their carefully smoothed woolen blankets and red-checked spreads that everyone thought how nice it would be to lie down in one of them for a minute.

"Right next door here I'll put in a small kitchen later on. A real tiny one, like in dining cars. The other end of the car will make another bedroom, and in the middle there'll be space enough for a fine living room," Matthias explained. He had thought it all out very carefully.

"Why, a whole family could live here," shouted Andrea, who was sweeping through the railroad car like a whirlwind, dragging Lenchen along behind her, and every now and then uttering high, clear little bird-cries of sheer joy. "Oh, I like it. Look at those sweet beds. Like at the seven dwarfs' house only there aren't seven. Finish it quick, Matthias, so that we can all move in with you."

"I'm sure Mrs. Almut would love that," Mother said. "And you've just promised Mrs. Verduz that you'll be the joy and sunshine of her old age."

"That's true," Andrea said. "It would be sad for her if she didn't have me. She's already said that she doesn't enjoy her coffee unless she has me around to talk to . . ." Suddenly Andrea stopped prancing, her eyes grew even larger than they normally were, and she said, "Holy smoke, now I know what it is. Noah's Ark!"

"Of course!" Margret was as excited by the idea as Andrea. "You're right, it's Noah's Ark keeping afloat when everything else has gone under. Oh, Mat, we must name our house Noah's Ark."

The very next day Matthias found a good smooth board and Joseph dug up a can of old oil paint for him. Together they painted NOAH'S ARK in big handsome letters on the board. The sign was nailed up over the door, much to the amusement of everybody on Rowan Farm. And Mrs. Almut said, "You're quite right—it's going to be your ark to carry you over the rough seas of these times."

The warm March days proved to be a false spring, and the weather reverted to bitter winter once more. In the biting cold it was not easy to get out of one's warm bunk at six and go across to the barn to do chores. Matthias had to clean out the manure and feed the animals while Margret milked. If only she could learn to milk. Every day she sat down on the three-legged milking stool beneath the cow's great, swelling side and tried again. Often the cow switched her tail

angrily and turned her head in annoyance to see who was
pulling and plucking so clumsily at her udder. Not a drop of
milk came out; a cow can do wonders in the way of holding
her milk back when she pleases.

Margret tried her hardest, but the more she tried the less
success she had. And on top of getting no milk there was that
awful cramp in her hands and a knife-sharp pain running up
to her shoulders, as though her arms were about to break
off. For a while each morning Mrs. Almut would stand by
and watch Margret's vain attempts. "You just have to keep
on trying every day," she would say. "It will come, all of a
sudden." And then she would gently move the girl aside and
sit down on the stool herself. At once the milk began hissing
into the pail and a thick foam appeared on top, just as it
should.

The four cows were such friendly animals that Margret
could not understand how they could put her to shame this
way. Margret always slipped an armful of fresh hay into their
mangers, although they had actually had their ration already,
and she would pat them and talk coaxingly to them. The
matron of the herd was Homann's Betsy. She had been
bought from a farmer named Homann who had the reputa-
tion of raising good stock. She was the mother of the herd
and had to be treated with a certain amount of deference.
Her two daughters, Carla and Jo, and Hulda, the black-and-
white, had to wait modestly until she was finished being
milked. Her highness was quite willing to let Margret scratch
her between her horns or under her chin. At such times she
was very amiable. But when it came to letting down her
milk, she began kicking her hind legs at the pail, switching
Margret in the face with her tail, and in general behaving

savagely. Of course the younger members of the herd imitated her. Fortunately Betsy was not going to be milking long; she was due to calve and would be dried off soon.

Milking was such a trial to Margret that she was heartily relieved to learn that at least the milk sheep were not being milked, since they would be lambing any day now. Margret was in sole charge of the sheep, so that Joseph and Matthias were left free for other work. In any case, looking after animals was the branch of farming which most interested her. Three times a day she went to look after her sheep—early in the morning, at noon, and in the evening when they were fed, for there was no feed for them outside now. All summer long and late into the fall they were out grazing on the moor where the cows could not find enough. Even now they were out in their yard all day long, but at night they were brought into their shed. Margret always spread fresh straw for them.

Just before going to bed she made a practice of looking in on them once more. They were big, strong animals, three ewes and Emil the ram, who usually wandered about the enclosure alone with a sulky expression on his face, for at this season the females did not want to have anything to do with him. Milk sheep are not herd animals like sheep which are kept for meat or wool. They were a rarity in this section of Germany. Before the war Mrs. Almut had gotten her first breeding pair from Holstein, and she had done well with the animals. Nowadays her lambs were eagerly bought, because the sale of sheep's milk was not hedged in by government regulations. Besides, it contained more butterfat than the richest cow milk.

Margret had made friends with the sheep right away. When she came into the shed at night and switched on the light, the three ewes, Belinda, Chloe and Phyllis, turned their heads toward her and greeted her with soft, bleating sounds. Even Emil, who was locked up alone in a box stall, mumbled contentedly and eagerly took a juicy beet she held out to him. Margret would feel to see whether any of the ewe's udders were swollen; that was how you told whether they were about to lamb. "As soon as you notice any change, call me," Mrs. Almut had told Margret.

It was necessary to keep an eye on Ate, too, now. From her first day Margret had wooed the dog, but Ate's friendship was not as easy to win as that of the sheep. She had been separated from her offspring and now spent most of her time lying in her kennel, whimpering softly whenever Mrs. Almut crossed the yard. In her present condition the dog seemed to need human company very badly. Margret fed her and walked her a little every day. She often sat down beside her and talked to her. And at last the day came when Ate of her own accord ran along behind Margret across the yard and followed her into the Ark.

"Can't I take her right in with me?" Margret asked Mrs. Almut. "Matthias could make a good big box for her. I'd put her in my room. Then she'd be nice and warm all the time and I'd notice right away if anything started happening at night. There's space enough; Matthias already has his own bedroom at the other end of the Ark."

"That will be fine," Mrs. Almut said. "You'll see how quickly Ate will become attached to you. And she must, because otherwise she won't let you touch her whelps and I want you to take care of this whole litter by yourself."

"But can't I call you just this time when she's ready?" Margret asked somewhat anxiously.

"Of course call me. But there's nothing to worry about if it's a normal birth. Ate is an experienced mother; she's already had four litters. Other females I've had insisted on being alone when they whelped. Every one is different."

So Ate moved into the Ark. Matthias had meanwhile put in electric lights. That was easy, since the line already ran from the horse stable to the sheep shed. With Joseph's help he had rigged up a branch circuit within a couple of hours. An old lamp and two outlets were found in Mrs. Almut's attic room. But there were no bulbs and these were almost impossible to get. However, Lenchen helped them out. She broached the subject to her father—and there were few things a butcher could not obtain these days. Next Sunday Andrea and Lenchen came out to the farm to visit and brought with them a small box containing two carefully packed bulbs. They were showered with praise and thanks. And since they were girls, they were even allowed to watch while Lumpi was fed. Margret had also taken over this job, because the men simply did not understand how to handle Lumpi. But the stallion took to Margret as thoroughly as she took to him. When he caught sight of her he would come trotting up and nudge her lovingly with his wet nose. He poked in her pockets for sugar and nibbled gently at her ear, without ever hurting her. This was the animal whom Joseph called "wicked"!

One night when Margret went into the sheep shed, accompanied by Ate, Chloe's and Belinda's udders felt hard and hot. She ran breathlessly to the house and told Mrs. Almut, who came back with her and decided that they would have to watch through the night with the sheep. Margret was to take turns with Matthias, and they would call Mrs. Almut herself as soon as the time came. She wanted to lie down and catch a few hours' sleep, for she had been up and about all day collecting wild seedlings for the nursery stock. The ewe Belinda was already lying on her side, breathing heavily; she was unwilling to get up. "It will probably take until tomorrow morning, though," Mrs. Almut said.

Matthias watched through the first half of the night. But even before the clock struck one Margret was up, much too restless to sleep. Ate lay peacefully in her box and wagged her tail as Margret bent over to look at her once more. No, there was no need to worry about Ate.

It was icy outside even though she had dressed warmly. But inside the sheep shed it was very snug. Matthias was sitting beside Chloe, on his knees a book on astronomy that the professor had lent him. But after his hard day's work he had already dozed off once or twice and he was glad when Margret turned up ahead of time to relieve him. "Good luck," he said to Margret as she sat down on the stool and wrapped her woolen blanket around her legs. "I think it will be starting soon."

"Has she been groaning hard?" Margret asked.

"Sometimes, and she's restless, standing up and then lying down again, and keeps turning her head to look at her tail. I moved her to the maternity box about ten."

"Good night, Matthias."

"Good night, Margret."

Margret bent over Chloe and stroked her nose. Once she got up to look at Belinda and Phyllis. It seemed to her that Belinda's turn would be coming very soon, but Phyllis was chewing her cud, peacefully and sleepily.

The wind soughed through the pines outside with the

low, deep note of an organ. Margret stepped to the door of the shed and looked up at the flickering stars. Two days ago the moon had been full and it now stood bright in the western sky. She felt very tired, but quite wide awake. When she stepped back into the stall again, a damp, sticky mass lay beside Chloe, who was poking her nose busily into it. Oh dear, Margret thought, with constricted heart—the lamb has been born dead. It was her fault—she hadn't been paying attention. Those few minutes she'd spent looking out had been fatal. But how could it have happened so unbelievably fast? She bent down, and suddenly something moved inside the wet sac. A tiny nose pushed through, a little mouth gasped for air; a series of kicks released first one miniature hoof and then another. The mother began busily licking the wretched little heap. Margret took a handful of clean straw and helped to rub the lamb dry. She was so excited that her hands shook.

A quarter of an hour later the newborn creature no longer looked so ugly. It was no longer wet and bedraggled; its tender hide was clothed in thousands of woolly curls, and it had a little tuft of wool above its sweet, foolish-looking baby face. At times it bleated angrily at the inhospitable world it had entered, and then the ewe would bleat reassuringly and pass her tongue over her baby.

"A handsome lamb," Margret praised her. "You have a beautiful baby, Chloe, and now I have to run and tell Mrs. Almut."

When she returned with Mrs. Almut, Chloe's second lamb had just been born. Chloe seemed to make a point of being alone at the critical moment. Together they rubbed it with straw and watched while the mother licked it off. Then they sat and waited to see whether there would be a third. "I doubt it," Mrs. Almut said. "These two are so big and strong it's hardly likely there will be another. But you can never tell. Milk sheep sometimes have as many as four lambs."

It was quiet and warm in the stall, the air filled with the strong animal smell. The newborn creatures bleated with tinny little voices until the mother got up to let them suck. The first-born was already standing, although none too steadily. Now the second struggled to his feet also. Margret guided them to their mother, and with eager bleats they butted their comical little heads against the swollen udder. There was a surprising vitality in the little creatures. In a moment they realized what had to be done to get at the warm, sweet milk. They began sucking greedily and swiftly, their stubby tails dancing gaily up and down.

"They're better at milking than you are," Mrs. Almut said.

"Now I know why you have to knead and pat the udder when you milk; the young do the same. Listen to the way they smack their lips. Oh, Mrs. Almut, isn't it marvelous?"

"It is!" Mrs. Almut said. "People who don't feel the marvel ought to let animals alone. Nothing does well if you don't put your heart into it. Even the soil feels whether you like it or not."

Margret nodded. She was happy to hear Mrs. Almut speak in this way to her. It was as if she had passed a test and received an award.

"Are you very homesick?" Mrs. Almut asked suddenly.

"I think about Mummy and the others a good deal."

"No, I mean homesick for your old home, where you came from."

At first Margret did not answer. At last she said, "I had

a twin brother. It wouldn't be any good going back, with him gone."

Mrs. Almut nodded. She patted one of the lambs. "That's so," she said. "That's the way it is when what you loved best departs. There's a long time afterwards when you're never at home anywhere. But wait, the dead come back. They come to life again within us; we only have to have patience and let it happen."

They sat in silence for a long time, until in the next stall Belinda cried plaintively. Chloe was lying peacefully, the two lambs pressed against the warm curve of her woolly belly, satiated and content. "I'll look to Belinda," Margret said. She went to the other stall and Belinda rubbed her head pleadingly against her leg. "She'll start soon," Margret said.

Within the next hour Belinda had three lambs, two of them strong and vigorous, but the third so weak that Margret had to peel it out of the slippery sac. The mother turned her head away, refusing to "own" it.

"The poor little cripple," Mrs. Almut said. "Joseph will have to kill it at once."

But Margret went on rubbing it harder than ever. "It isn't a cripple at all," she said. "It's perfectly all right, just a little weak." She looked pleadingly at Mrs. Almut. "It must live. Please, please let it live."

"If you've set your heart on it, we'll wait a few days and see. But you'll have your work cut out for you."

"Oh, thank you," Margret said. "What a hard-hearted mother Belinda is. Look how sweet it is, now that I've got it dry. Here, Belinda, look at it and let it drink. Come, my baby, drink nicely, nobody's going to hurt you."

The pens had to be cleaned after it was all over. Then Margret spread fresh straw while Mrs. Almut lit a fire in the kitchen so that she could prepare warm gruel for the animals.

"And now lie down until eight o'clock," she said to Margret when they left the shed together at five in the morning. And Margret was certainly grateful for her bed in the warm little bedroom of the Ark.

Three hours' sleep was not very much. Margret was still reeling with weariness when she returned to the sheep shed at eight. She found everything in perfect order. Belinda's youngest lamb lay beside the two others, close up to its mother, obviously accepted into the family circle. But Margret would have to watch out and make sure it received enough milk and was not pushed away from the udder by its stronger sisters. Margret let it drink again until it was satiated; then she had to hurry out to attend to her other work. There was so much to do. Kathrin had meanwhile fed the chickens and the pig, and for a change had milked also— because Mrs. Almut had to go out early that morning in the rattletrap of a farm truck to pick up the milk cans of all the farms round about and deliver them to the collecting station at Hellborn.

Margret cleaned the chickenhouse quickly. Then the stairs and hallway in the house had to be swept and Mrs. Almut's room done up. Kathrin wanted potatoes peeled and the dogs were already standing with their heads pressed against the kennel fence, waiting for their walk. They had to be brushed first, and Margret fooled around with them a bit because they were looking so sad and reproachful. Ate, too, needed a bit of exercise; it would be good for her, but she had to be taken out alone now. Margret walked her a short distance down the highway. A jeep drove past them and turned in at Rowan Farm. That must be the American captain who bought Alf, Margret thought. He would come along just when I had no sleep all night and Mrs. Almut will be gone until noon.

She hurried back to the yard, where she found the American waiting at the kennel gate. Ate growled crossly, as though she suspected that the captain wanted to carry off one of her sons. Margret had to hold the dog tightly by the collar.

"Morning," the American said, throwing an amused look at the long-legged girl who frowningly returned his gaze. "Nobody home?"

"I am," Margret said. "I'm the kennel maid here. I suppose you've come for your dog?"

"The kennel maid!" the driver called from his seat in the jeep. "Isn't she cute?"

"Yes, the kennel maid," Margret said in English. She was not going to have them think she didn't understand English. Not for nothing had her father and mother had the whole family reading and practicing English—in the good old days when they were all together.

"Let's look at the dogs," the captain said, switching to English. His German was a little on the rough side. "Hello, Alfy. He's the handsomest, isn't he?"

"You're mistaken, that's Arjopa," Margret said. What a funny man. He didn't even recognize the dog he had picked out a few weeks ago. "That one over there is Alf, and he certainly is better-looking."

"Haha," the captain laughed. She seemed to amuse him

tremendously. "So Alf is the better-looking because I've bought him. You're a real little businessman."

Margret only shrugged.

"But the other one looks better to me," the captain went on. "Come over here, Lincoln. Which do you like better?"

"That one," the chauffeur said, pointing to Arjopa.

"And the kid is trying to tell me the other one is better."

Margret was beginning to get good and angry. "If you like Arjopa better, you can have him instead."

"Fine!" the captain said. "Here, I promised Mrs. Almut this." He took a large can of coffee from the jeep and handed it to Margret. "Hop in, Arjopa. Bye-bye. Be seeing you."

He tucked the dog between his knees, holding fast to the collar, and waved. The jeep roared off. He was awfully fresh, Margret thought, but really quite nice. And now he has the dog he wants and I have the one I want. But she was a little worried about what Mrs. Almut would say.

As soon as the rattling, ancient pick-up drove into the yard, Margret ran up to Mrs. Almut and told her the story. "You're a fine one," Mrs. Almut said. "Here less than a month and doing business on your own already. These things might turn out badly, my girl. But you've probably done right this time. How is your little cripple? Still alive?"

"It's alive all right," Margret said.

"Then I'll give it to you," Mrs. Almut called from the door of the house. Margret was already on her way back to the sheep shed, for it was time to set the little lamb to sucking again. "If you can keep it alive, it's yours."

Margret felt like doing a somersault out of sheer pride and joy. If only she weren't so frightfully tired. The day seemed to go on forever. But that night she got up twice to look after her lamb. Toward three o'clock in the morning, when she came out for the second time, the little "cripple" was actually standing and sucking from its mother all by itself, and its belly was round as a little drum. "I don't have to get up at night any more to see to you," Margret said, and she put her arms tightly around the lamb. Its nose was all smeared with milk and its voice sounded content and well-fed. "You sweet darling, you. I'm going to call you Rachel, understand. That's the only Old Testament name I can think of right now, and it has to be something from the Old Testament because you're the first animal in our Noah's Ark."

On Fridays, when dog meat had to be fetched, Matthias and Margret often drove into town by themselves because Mrs. Almut had so much else to do. They felt like kings as they drove down the highroad behind the trotting ponies. Usually they were frozen through, but they would not have changed places with anyone. Young as they were, they were people of responsibility—and that was something! They got the meat from the slaughterhouse, exchanged a few serious, grown-up comments with the inspector, conscientiously carried out all errands, and always made a quick trip over to Parsley Street to see their mother. They ate their lunch there and had a cup of hot coffee with Mother.

"Imagine, I have a sheep, a sheep all my own!" Margret told her mother the first Friday after the birth of the lambs. "I'm going to learn to spin, and then we'll have knitting wool. It's about time, too, because my stockings are nothing but holes."

"The foundation of your own herd!" her mother replied. "Goodness, you've come a long way. But I have some news too. No, you'll never guess. Imagine, our treasure hunters have actually found something."

"I can't believe it!" Matthias cried. "Have they really found a treasure?"

"No, not exactly a treasure, but a locked suitcase. They dug through piles of rubble back of the mysterious door, and you can imagine the state they got their clothes into. Of course they wanted to break the suitcase right open at home, but I didn't let them. You should have heard their howls when I insisted they take it to the police."

"Did I hear police?" Matthias asked as if he did not believe his ears.

"To the police?" Margret groaned. "But, Mummy, who knows what was in it. Once the police have their hands on it, we can just say good-by to anything in it."

"Children, children! Someone may need it badly. And if no one comes to claim it, we'll get it back in a year."

"A year is so awfully long. Nobody but you would ever have thought of taking it to the police."

"Too bad, if that's the case. Anyway, the police sergeant took down a deposition. Preposition, Joey called it; you should have seen Joey all swollen with importance. Then the boys were asked whether they wanted to waive their claim to the finder's reward, and they said No at the top of their voices. The sergeant laughed and said he just had to ask because that was regulations, and he also had to ask if they wanted to renounce their property right in case no one called for the suitcase. Then they shouted No even louder than before, and Hans Ulrich looked at the deposition and said, "Make sure you write that down right." The sergeant promised he would. Then he said he thought he knew the owner of the suitcase, and they would hear from him.

"Have they heard yet?"

"Of course not. All this happened just the day before yesterday."

"You'll never hear anything more about it," Matthias predicted grimly.

"Don't be so mistrustful," Mother said. "Sometimes honesty is really rewarded."

"Oh, Mummy," Margret sighed, kissing her. "You're so hopelessly old-fashioned—you ought to be re-educated. Good-by, Mummy. Write us a note if anything happens."

When they came home, Ate had just begun to whelp. Margret had hardly expected it today, because the dog had been so gay and frisky in the morning. She quickly put on her kennel apron and sat down beside Ate. Ate raised her head and uttered a soft cry of complaint. "Have they left you all alone, poor thing?" Margret consoled her. "Don't worry, now I'm here with you and I won't leave." Contentedly, the dog laid her head on Margret's knee and looked trustfully up at her out of her beautiful, chestnut-brown eyes.

Five healthy whelps came into the world without any difficulty. Margret had full responsibility, because Mrs. Almut was not yet back. Toward evening Ling, the Chinese, came to look for Margret, who had not come to supper. Ate growled, and he stayed at a respectful distance from her, holding out a steaming bowl of soup that he had brought. "How kind of you, Ling," Margret said. "Thank you very much." Now, with the food before her, she realized how hungry she was and got up to eat. But at once Ate began whining pitifully.

"She doesn't want me to leave," Margret said, and she sat down on the edge of Ate's box with the bowl on her knees.

"Ling get stlaw," the Chinese said, and went over to the barn. Margret was relieved, for she would need fresh straw.

Much later, when the five fat little balls were all clinging contentedly to their mother's teats, Margret stole away to fetch warm milk for the dog. Ate wagged her tail happily when she returned and gratefully lapped up the milk. At last, when Margret hesitantly and cautiously made a move to pick up one of the pups, Ate lifted her paw, looked up at Margret with unlimited trust and permitted her children to be examined one after the other.

A few days later the rural mail carrier brought a letter to Miss Margret Lechow on Rowan Farm. It was from Andrea.

Dear Margret, [Andrea wrote,] something perfectly *unbelievable* has happened. You'll never guess what it is. The treasure hunters have found a suitcase with nothing but paper in it. But it isn't ordinary paper; the police say it belongs to a lady who needs it. I don't know what for. Not for starting fires, you know—it's paper with *something on it*. The inspector said, "You're in luck. This stuff is worth more than gold." Have you ever heard anything like that? And you know what goes with it? *A big reward.* The lady it belongs to is sick now but when she gets better the boys are going to see her. They're swell-headed and famous on Parsley Street and Mrs. Verduz says she knew right away that Joey was a clever boy. That's an odd thing for her to say because I help her lots more than Joey. I hear you have a sheep and I'm coming to see it soon, does it come into the world all finished or just started like

Cosi's pups with those funny eyes and ears? I'm coming to see you soon because I can't stand it here any longer. Hans Ulrich and Joey are so swell-headed they won't listen to *anybody*. How is Noah's Ark? Will it soon be finished? Much love to you and Matthias. The sheep and the pups, are they sweet?

Your loving sister, Andrea.

P.S. The lady's name is Mrs. Hertrich and she has a factory. Joey is only getting half and he can't figure more than a hundred. He's promising everybody *all sorts of things,* but Margret, dear, maybe you don't need anything because you're earning your own money and Matthias too.

CHAPTER NINE

Spring

THE APRIL rain trickled softly down. It was the best of weather for planting. Joseph and Matthias were out in the fields all day, and the women worked in the small kitchen garden along the south side of the shed wall. To protect the garden from chickens, sheep, ponies and dogs, Mrs. Almut had surrounded it with a barbed-wire fence which was concealed behind a hedge of wild roses. Every year that hedge was full of birds' nests.

Margret stood stooped over in the rain. She thrust the dibble into the damp, dark earth with its spicy smell, lowered the white roots into the hole and pressed the earth tightly around them. She was setting out tomato and lettuce plants, and the gentle rain promptly watered them for her.

Matthias passed by on the other side of the hedge and looked over at her. Margret straightened up. The rain ran down over her face. She glanced with pleasure at the fresh green seedlings standing in orderly rows. "Waxing moon," she said to Matthias. "Plants set then grow best, Mrs. Almut says."

Matthias grinned. He and Joseph did not think much of waxing moons and suchlike superstitions.

"You don't have to grin like that," Margret said. "Ouch!" she groaned, and put her hand to her back. "For this work I ought to have a back of iron with a hinge in it."

"I've wished I had the same more than once," Matthias said comfortingly. "I'm going to the mill. Will you come along?"

Margret did not need a second invitation. "I have to get some barley ground—the chicks are going to hatch soon. If we drive across the fields, Fury and Alf can run along. Look, they're standing at the kennel gate stretching their necks and suspecting I've forgotten their walk. I'll hurry—whistle when you get the horses hitched up."

When the last plant was set, she ran across the yard to take a quick look at Ate. She lay stretched out on the big overhanging roof of the kennel, so that the whelps who already had sharp little milk teeth could not continually pester her. After the raw March days were past and the little pups had opened their eyes, Margret had moved them to the part of the kennel which had always been used for a nursery. Now they stood, crying out in comical little yowls and growls and peering up at their big mother who had so heartlessly deserted them.

"It's high time we registered them in the breeder's book," Mrs. Almut had told Margret a few days ago. "Think up some nice names for them. It's the B's turn. And then fill out the small forms you'll find in the left-hand drawer of my desk. What have I got a kennel maid for?" Mrs. Almut hated all filling out of forms and keeping books. What she liked best was going out with the ponies or riding around in her old rattletrap of a truck. "Everywhere and nowhere," Kathrin would growl. "That's the way she's always been." But Mrs. Almut said she had to keep up contacts with people, visit other breeders, go to shows, look at other nurseries. These things were as necessary as the work on the farm.

"B,B,B," Margret murmured thoughtfully as she brushed Ate. Dogs born in the Ark by rights should have had Biblical names, but Margret did not imagine she could find five Biblical names beginning with B. "Birch," she thought, looking at the fair, sleek little female. The two males might be called Battak and Bayard, the two golden-yellow females Bona and Bashka. Bashka was the one who would probably stay in the kennel. She had the finest color and a deep black mask extending over her eyes. The head, too, promised well. But it was always dangerous to judge dogs too early; better to hold on to them as long as possible.

The rain had stopped. A keen breeze was blowing down from the mountains and sweeping the clouds together like a huge broom. Abruptly, the sky grew clear and blue as though it had been washed clean. Cherries and plum trees were already beginning to bloom on the slopes. It seemed as though everything were bursting into doubly luxuriant growth after the unusual severity of the winter. The April sun blazed down upon the wet mowings, and every blade of grass sparkled as though hung with gems. In the fields the puddles between the plow-ridges reflected the gold of the sun and the blue of the sky.

Fury and Alf leaped and rushed about madly as soon as Margret let them out of the kennel. The ponies, too, were full of spring pep and trotted fast, manes streaming, down the road that led across the fields.

The village was swarming with children, and once again the battles between the farm children and the refugee children were in progress. These battles never stopped. Neither the children nor the parents of the opposing groups could get along. Nobody liked the strangers who took space and food away from old and settled inhabitants. "The beggars," the farmers called them, never thinking that the refugees too had once owned houses and farms, workshops and stores, and that they had been driven away from their rightful homes. The refugees had never guessed that someday they would have to beg for the barest necessities.

"The hardhearted farmers," the strangers said, refusing to understand how hard it is to have your house filled up with people you don't know, to have to move into fewer rooms, no longer to be master in your own home after it has survived years of bombings.

It was as though someone had cast an evil spell upon them, so that each group saw the other in a distorted light, each thought the other existed only to make a difficult life even harder.

Margret and Matthias felt little of this constant antagonism in the friendly atmosphere of Rowan Farm. But when they came into the village they noticed resentful looks. And more than once they had heard spiteful remarks about Mrs. Almut. No wonder the woman's place wouldn't prosper, someone said, when she had nothing better to do than to take up with refugees, without even being ordered to.

As Margret and Matthias drove up to the mill and unloaded their sacks, the miller came out and curtly answered their greeting. "Are you still with Mrs. Almut?" he asked.

"Why shouldn't we be?" Matthias replied quietly.

The miller watched as they lifted the heavy sacks. "Oh yes," he said, "old lady Almut with her experiments. Dog breeding and horse raising and milk-sheep—what's going to be the end of it? And Bernd still away. Who knows whether he'll ever come back?" He wagged his head morosely. At bottom he liked Mrs. Almut, as did almost all the people in the village, although they always had some criticism to make of her.

"Bring the sacks in here," the miller said. "There. What do you want to have?"

"One bag of wheat flour and one of rye," Matthias said.

"And barley grits," Margret added. "And then I wanted to ask whether you couldn't roll a sack of oats for me one of these days. I need oatmeal badly for my pups."

"Oatmeal for dogs? Who ever heard the like! Oh, all right, bring me a sack of oats when you come by, it's all the same to me."

"What an unfriendly man," Margret said to Matthias as they drove slowly back up the hill.

"Oh, he's not as mean as he acts," Matthias answered. "His grumbling doesn't mean much. What bothers me is that he gives us short weight. But there's nothing you can do; Mrs. Almut says you can't afford to be on bad terms with the only miller in the village. He knows where he stands and makes a good profit out of it."

As they drove through the village they saw an old woman coming from the direction of Mariazell. A swarm of children was trailing after her, singing something that seemed to be directed against her, for she kept turning around and raising her stick threateningly. Whenever she did, the band would scatter, screeching, only to reassemble again.

As the cart came up to her, she lifted her hand, asking for a ride. Matthias stopped the ponies and Margret reached down. The old woman grasped her hand and scrambled nimbly up to the box. She had stiff grey hair that the wind blew in streamers around her head, and a pair of large, dark brown, wild-looking eyes.

"Do you live up there, too?" Margret asked.

"Right back of the woods," the woman said. "Don't you know me?"

"No. Yes, I think I've seen you crossing the yard."

"I know you well, girlie; many's the time I've peeked into the cowstall when you sat trying to milk and not getting a drop. It goes better now, don't it?"

"Oh yes, I can do it pretty well now."

"I'll tell you what, you have to sing while milkin'. The cows like it and the sheep too. You try that. And in June come to my house and dig yourself some St. John's wort and carry it in your pocket. That makes all animals obey you. And hang some of the blossom in the stable to protect the beasts from hexing. It's good for scours, too. You just ask old Marri. Whoa, I get out here. God bless you and give Annie Almut my regards, but not Kathrin, that old scarecrow."

The children turned in to the road leading to Rowan Farm. The dogs ran on ahead and barked at the gate so that Joseph came to open it and help them unload their sacks. Mrs. Almut came out of the house too and began unhitching the ponies, who rubbed their noses against her and nudged at her pockets looking for bread. In place of her usual shaggy winter hat she was wearing a cap made of an old stocking which kept her bobbed hair from being too much tossed by the wind.

"An old woman asked us to give you her regards," Margret said. "Her name is Marri and the village kids were running after her."

"She's the one the village calls the bee witch," Mrs. Almut said. "You mean to say you haven't heard about her or run into her before? She comes by here often, though Kathrin raises a fuss every time and throws salt over her shoulder if she as much as sets eyes on her. Years ago, when we first came here, Marri had her little cabin right back of our woods. She lived there with her son. He was just a little older than my Bernd. He isn't living now, and since he was killed his mother has gotten queerer and more of a hermit even than she used to be."

"But why do people call her a witch?" Margret asked. "And why does Kathrin throw salt over her shoulder?"

"Ask her yourself, there she is," Mrs. Almut said.

Kathrin was there all right, standing at the door of the house and already in a temper. "Who was it that you took in the cart? The bee witch? Holy saints and Saviour, are you clean out of your head? Want her to make the horses lame? Want her to hex weevils in all our flour, the old hag?"

"But she didn't do anything of the sort—she just gave me some good advice," Margret objected. "You're being silly, Kathrin. There aren't things like witches."

"There aren't things like witches, you say? I suppose you know, still wet behind the ears like you are. So there aren't any witches. Did she ask you any questions? She started right off, didn't she? And if you say yes three times, then she's got you, she can do what she wants with you. Everybody in the village knows that. Oh my Heavens, how can you kids be so ignorant?"

All the rest of that day Margret thought about the old woman who lived alone in the woods and was considered a witch. As she was milking she recalled what Marri had said. Sitting on the three-legged stool and gently caressing and kneading Jo's full udder, she began singing softly, "I want none of your weevily wheat and I want none of your barley," and milking to the tempo of the song. Was it only her imagination or was the milk really flowing faster into the pail? At any rate, all four cows turned their heads to look at her, and Jo did not switch her tail the way she always used to. When the milking was done there was a heavy foam on top of the pail, and Margret made up her mind to report this to the old woman the next time she met her.

At supper she asked, "Why is Marri called the bee witch?"

"Why, because she steals people's swarms by bewitching them," Kathrin said maliciously. "How else would she always have the best swarms and the most honey?"

"Because she knows something about beekeeping, that's all," Mrs. Almut said. "You ought to see how she handles her bees, and all the bee forage she's set out in her garden and round about. Summers her little place is a mass of flowers."

"But . . . is she bad? Is that why people are afraid of her?"

"Nonsense, she's just different from other people. She never does anyone any harm, but she's still a stranger here after thirty years, and she's had a hard life. It's the others who are bad, the people who say nasty things about her, and they're stupid and superstitious besides. Our pastor has often criticized them for it. And you, Kathrin, if you are as good a Christian as you pretend, you ought not to say such silly things."

Offended, Kathrin took her plate and shuffled into the kitchen, mumbling dark prophesies of the misfortunes that would come over the farm if she were not heeded.

The children got up from table soon afterward, for now that the evenings were still light they could get in quite a bit of work on the Ark. Since Margret and Matthias each had a bedroom to themselves, Dieter could share Matthias' room when he came out to help on Sundays, and for Whitsuntide Mrs. Almut had invited Mother and the rest of the family. Margret was looking forward to this visit so hard she could scarcely wait. She was making curtains out of some old bedspreads, gay, red-checked curtains that matched the beds perfectly. Ate would be able to sleep in Margret's room again as soon as the whelps no longer needed her. Then Alf would guard the yard, Fury the house and Ate the Ark. Rowan Farm was lucky to have watchdogs in these unsettled times.

"We need beds for our visitors," Margret said to Matthias that night. "Can't we put in another bunk above each of ours? There are always upper and lower berths in railroad cars."

"Not a bad idea," Matthias said. "Yes, let's. But we have to figure out a way to support the upper bunks so they won't collapse as soon as someone lies down in them."

"Oh, Otto the blacksmith can make us one of those things you screw on, you know, a sort of angle thing. We can pay him with some Rhode Island hatching eggs; I remember that his wife would like to have a few. Those old biddies of hers don't lay very well. You know, Matthias, I'd like to get some new life into chicken farming all over the country."

"Silly. The farm women would give you a quick brush-off if you tried to tell them anything. But let's think about what to do with our Ark. Look, how about putting two berths one above the other along each wall, and in that way the two compartments will sleep eight people. And then along the windows we'll build a coffer bench for storing things."

"As if we had anything to store."

"Well, you have to be prepared for everything. Now hold this board firm so I can saw it . . . there . . . Dieter's coming again next Sunday, and Joseph said he'd pipe water from the horse barn over to the Ark. He has to dig up some lead pipe somewhere. Hans has promised to get us a batch of bricks. We'll use them to build a chimney for the tile stove in the living room. I've figured it all out. And then we'll put a bench around the stove . . ."

"What plans you have! Why do we need a cookstove when we always eat at Mrs. Almut's?"

"You can never tell," Matthias said. "There. Now hold the molding on it, but keep it straight, please." He placed the nail in position and hit it squarely on the head. "Nails," he groaned. "If only we had enough nails. I've pulled nails out of all the old boards in the woodshed and hammered them straight. And screws. Can you imagine that people once used to go straight into a store and buy a box of screws?"

Dusk had fallen while they worked. The brother and sister stood quietly for a while in front of the Ark and watched the slender sickle of the moon rising over the mountains. The April night was so clear that the pines near the Ark and the fruit trees in the pasture stood out against the sky like silhouettes cut out of black paper. Every branch was distinct.

"How beautiful Jupiter is over there," Matthias said. "If only I could get another look at him through a good telescope and see his moons. And there's Cassiopeia, see the big W."

Margret nodded. "Better go in to bed, Matthias," she said. "You have to relieve Joseph in the barn at one o'clock."

"Do you think Homann's Betsy will have a heifer calf?"

"Let's hope so. I'll look in on the dogs once more. Good night."

Margret fetched Ate from the kennel and took one more walk with her as far as the stone bench. In the professor's room the lamp was still burning. On one of the neighboring farms a dog barked. Ate pricked up her ears, but none of the Rowan Farm dogs answered.

Margret thought of old Marri living completely alone in the woods. She ought to have a dog so that she would not be without protection. But then Margret thought of something the professor had said recently: "Do not heap up precious goods and you need fear no thief." That was a consolation. The little old woman had surely not accumulated anything that would attract robbers.

"Come, Ate!" Margret said. The big beast sprang to her side at once and pressed its head against her arm. How peaceful everything was, peaceful and sheltered in the stillness of a spring evening—the sleeping animals and the cow waiting for her calf; Mrs. Almut, waiting patiently for a son who for all anyone knew might never return. And brown Laura sitting on her eggs. The whole farm, with its woods

and fields and garden and the young seedlings she had set
today; and the lonely old woman with her bees on the other
side of the woods. Even the dead were wrapped in this
peace, even Christian and black Cosi. They no longer lay
under the apple tree in far-away Pomerania. They were here,
and their being here with her was more real than their death.

CHAPTER TEN

Big Things from
a Small Suitcase

THE BOYS were bubbling with excitement on the day they were to meet Mrs. Hertrich, the owner of the suitcase. Hans Ulrich had come home with Joey right after school, and now they stood over the tub of warm water and washed themselves so energetically that Andrea was prompted to call out:

"Great events cast their shadows before." As an afterthought, she added, "Don't forget your ears."

The reminder was really not necessary. They had already, Joey assured her, washed their "whole face and behind the ears and even the back of the neck," not to speak of their hands. Now they combed their hair with water and stood for a long time in front of the mirror, trying to part their hair straight as an arrow. They polished their shoes until they shone as much as old and hard-worn shoes could possibly shine, and they brushed their jackets until Mrs. Lechow was afraid the thin material would fall apart.

Their appointment was for four, but by three they were

standing around, all ready, begging Mother to hurry and get her coat on. On the way they talked incessantly of what they were going to say to the "suitcase lady." Above all she must be made to realize that it had been no easy matter to work through those remnants of wall and get the door clear and then open. They had squeezed through, but no grownup could have made it. Even now that it was all over Mother's hair stood on end when she heard how the treasure hunt had been conducted.

The house where the suitcase was found was not Mrs. Hertrich's. She lived in a large house near the big factory in the suburbs which had belonged to her husband and now belonged to her son. And since everyone expected that the factory would be one of the first places to be bombed, she had given the suitcase containing papers and a few valuable jewels to her daughter, whose home was near a school. Houses in that vicinity, presumably, would be safe from bombing. But like so many things, it had turned out differently from what people expected. The bombs had fallen on the house near the school and not on the factory. Later Mrs. Hertrich's daughter with her two children and several other people had been dug out of the ruins, but they were dead and could not account for the suitcase.

Mrs. Hertrich's house was very fine, full of rugs and mirrors and pretty pictures on the walls, highly-polished antique furniture and vases filled with spring flowers. The old lady sat in an armchair near the window awaiting her visitors. She greeted Mrs. Lechow pleasantly, and then greeted the boys who stood in front of her, scrutinizing the carpet and looking rather foolish, not a bit like heroic members of the guild of treasure-hunters.

"So you two found my suitcase," the lady said. "I'm very grateful to you."

"Oh, y'welcome," Joey said.

"Yes, y'welcome," Hans Ulrich said.

Mother took the chair which faced Mrs. Hertrich. Joey threw a pleading look at her, but she was not a bit helpful.

"I suppose it was a dangerous and difficult business getting down into that bombed cellar?" the lady asked.

"Oh, it wasn't bad," Hans Ulrich said.

"Not much to it," Joey said.

"And now I want to give you a reward. What would you like?"

At this point something very queer happened. It was almost like being in school when for a change they had really learned their lesson properly and then couldn't get the answer out when the teacher asked them. They shifted from one foot to the other, poked each other, turned red behind their cleanly-washed ears, and grinned.

At last Hans Ulrich took heart and said, "We wondered whether you made shoes in your factory."

"Or pants," Joey added.

The lady shook her head. She didn't manufacture either. The factory, alas, produced nothing more interesting than cement and cinder block. But she did not bring this up; perhaps she was ashamed to mention it. At any rate, she looked down at the carpet and saw the two pairs of boys' shoes. Joey's weren't so bad; they had once been a pair of good ski boots. Margret and Andrea had worn them before Joey, and they had done well by Joey's feet all through the family's long flight. But Hans Ulrich's shoes were really something to look at. The uppers were full of cracks. When rain ran into one hole it could easily run out again on the other side. Fortunately the soles were out of sight. And then Mrs. Hertrich's eyes passed upward from the shoes along the thin legs to the bare knees and the patched and repatched pants to Hans Ulrich's jacket. Her gaze climbed up a ladder of buttons, each one bearing not the slightest resemblance to any of the others. The jacket was buttoned right up to the neck, and there probably was a reason for that. Hans Ulrich's face grew even redder and he said, "Don't think I haven't any shirt. It's just that it didn't get dry in time."

Mrs. Hertrich looked at Mrs. Lechow. Then she took out her handkerchief and made a great business of rubbing her nose. When she put her handkerchief away again, it was quite clear that she was terribly unhappy because her factory did not make shoes and pants and shirts. But Hans Ulrich, who couldn't stand seeing people unhappy, said consolingly to her, "I wouldn't mind having a scooter."

Whereupon Joey was suddenly filled with courage and boldly reached for the sky. "A boy in our class has roller skates," he said.

But alas, that factory didn't seem to produce anything useful at all. "You know," the lady said, "suppose you go to play in the garden a bit. In a little while there'll be coffee and cake for you."

No second invitation was needed. Unfortunately the garden was not very amusing. Most of the flower beds were still mulched with pine branches. Only a small border near the house held some crocuses and blooming daffodils, but there was not much you could do with them, although they were pretty enough. Fortunately the boys found a small gate that led out into the factory yard. There two workmen in blue overalls were fixing a big truck, and they were handling all sorts of fascinating tools. The boys posted themselves nearby, addressed some bright remarks to the drivers, and were soon close friends of theirs. They were allowed to help and worked like beavers greasing the axles and mounting the tires. So on the whole it turned out to be an interesting afternoon, but just when they were having the time of their lives they were called in to coffee and realized too late that they no longer looked quite so clean as they had when they arrived.

Mother had meanwhile had a long conversation with Mrs. Hertrich, whose son later came over from the office and sat down with the ladies. When they heard Hans Ulrich's story, they said he must come to visit with them for a few weeks— it would give the skinny little fellow a chance to rest and fatten up. And if they liked him, they suggested, they might later adopt him.

"The thing to do first, though," Mrs. Hertrich said, "is to get those two boys some clothes." She suddenly became aware, with horror, of all the things she had laid up in boxes and chests in her attic. "We think much too much of ourselves and our own sorrow," she said. "We must help far more than we do."

"It's never too late for that," Mrs. Lechow answered with her warm smile. "If you want to help I can tell you about several families, good people all of them, where help is really needed."

She began talking about the old Lebenows in their damp cellar apartment without enough bedclothes; about Mrs. Krikoleit whose children could not go to school in winter because they had no shoes; about the Bennewitzes whose sick daughter had to share one bed with two well children; and the Millaus who had no warm clothes at all.

The old lady became very eager to distribute things. Mrs. Lechow had to go up to the attic with her at once and see what there was. And what bounty they found! There were suits of her husband's which did not fit her son, but would make wonderful Sunday clothes for Hans Ulrich and Joey. Mrs. Lechow stroked the fine, strong material lovingly. Then she burst out in a soft cry of delight when she came across two pairs of splendid riding breeches with leather-reinforced seats. They were officers' breeches of the last war, made of indestructible grey whipcord. There were also boots and shoes, and a lavender dress that could be fixed over for Margret, and a red one that would do for Andrea. In fact, the two ladies had as good a time over the chests filled with clothes and mothballs as the boys had had with the trucks. Both had red cheeks and shining eyes when they came downstairs with a laundry basket filled with things, and Mrs. Lechow happily promised to send the four women she had mentioned over in the morning. When they parted, Mrs. Hertrich's son said, "You must soon come again. My mother hasn't been so happy for years."

On the way home the boys plied Mother with questions. They carried the heavy laundry basket between them—that was a job they insisted on taking over, although they had to set the basket down often to rest. And Heaven be praised, they had found their lost tongues again.

"What's in the basket?" they wanted to know. "Shoes? Pants? And maybe socks, too, because we've about done for ours digging for the treasure. And we could use some shirts."

"You'll see when we get home. But how does it strike you, Hans Ulrich—you're going to pay a visit to those nice people and stay in the fine house for a while?"

"Do you think they'll let me ride in the truck?"

"You'll have to ask them," Mother said.

"I guess they won't send me out to the country to get potatoes."

"No, of course not. But what I like best of all is that you won't have to go stealing coal."

"That's too bad, I'm pretty good at that. I've never been caught."

"The basket's nice and heavy," Joey said. "If there's anything we can't use we can take it to the exchange center. The grocer got a pair of ee-normous snowshoes at the exchange center."

"Just think," Mother said. "If you work hard and study well they're going to send you to college some day."

"What's the idea?" the two boys asked in chorus. "We were supposed to get a *reward*."

But happily that part of the reward was far in the future, and for the moment they had much to rejoice in.

As soon as they got home, they started unpacking, with much whooping and shouting. Andrea could not get over her amazement that all these beautiful things which had lain in chests for scores of years should come to light just because of that tiny suitcase. "It was a good thing we took it to the police," she said thoughtfully.

And then she discovered the red woolen dress with the lace collar, and she put it on at once. The boys shouted and tittered at the sight of the thin beanpole of a girl inside the huge dress. Suddenly there was a knock at the door and Mrs.

Verduz stuck her pointed nose in. "I don't suppose I should, but if you don't mind, Mrs. Lechow," she said. And then she admired everything at length and wrung her hands and exclaimed how good it was that there were some people who kept their old things in such good order, and everyone agreed heartily with her. "If your blessed husband should see the things *you've* lent us," Andrea said, "he'd be very pleased up there in Heaven."

Mrs. Verduz was in a spot; she could not bear being considered any less generous than the fine lady who owned the suitcase. "Those things weren't just for loan," she said solemnly. "You are to keep them all. I am an old woman and my heirs are all well off. They won't be needing the few things I've given you."

"Everything?" Andrea asked prudently, giving Mrs. Verduz one of her angelic blue-eyed looks. "Even the silverware?"

"Even the silverware," Mrs. Verduz said. "Come, Caliph."

And then Mrs. Lechow sat down and sewed and sewed and sewed. The boys had to try things on until they were sick and tired of it. At times little disputes cropped up. The boys, for example, had their hearts set on short pants, as short as possible, which would be fine for summer. But Andrea and Lenchen maintained that Hans Ulrich's knees ought to be covered up. They were too bony to bear looking at. The boys just shrugged. What did girls know about style in boys' clothes. But Mother took the girls' side. "Of course we're going to make knickerbockers," Mother said. "They do for summer and winter both and they look better than anything else. Especially for *big* boys," she added.

Before long Hans Ulrich began his visit with the Hertrichs. It was almost unbelievable how well he was fixed. He had a little room all to himself. In it was a chest full of all sorts of toys and a bookcase filled with books. In rainy weather these things would probably be worth looking at, but now that it was spring there were other things to do. Hans Ulrich found a lot of occupation in the factory yard. He went on wonderful rides with the truck drivers—and after all he had a certain loyalty to his good old ruin. It was still a place of unlimited possibilities.

"Please don't crawl around in all those awful places," Mrs. Hertrich said. "I shudder to think of what could happen to the two of you there."

Luckily she did not know just how dangerous it was.

Joey, too, was soon an established visitor at the house, or at any rate at the factory yard. The biggest attraction was the truck drivers. You could learn an awful lot of useful things from them. "I'm going to be a truck driver when I grow up," Hans Ulrich said. "You don't have to go to college for that, Heini says."

Hans confided to his friend Joey that the Hertrichs made him bathe on Saturdays "up to the neck." But it wasn't really bad because the tub was so big you could play walrus in it and sail little boats on it, and no matter how much water you splashed on the floor, it just ran off and nobody scolded. "And at meals," he said, "gee it's funny, they don't even count and divide up the potatoes."

"Before long you'll be too spoiled to like visiting us," Andrea said.

But that was something Hans Ulrich could not conceive. "It's nicer here than anywhere else," he maintained.

Mrs. Lechow went to see Mrs. Hertrich at least once a week. The two women soon became good friends, and out of this friendship there flowed a steady stream of help and comfort to many families who had thought they had nowhere to turn.

One evening Joey put down his soup spoon and spoke up in sudden dismay. "The rest of us have got so much out of the suitcase, Mummy, that it's almost like a magic suitcase with everybody getting his wish and still it's never empty. Only we've forgotten all about you. You've got nothing out of it."

"Yes," Andrea said. "What awful brats we are. We've grabbed everything and left nothing over for our poor sweet Mummy."

But Mother looked serenely at her two awful brats, and then she said, "Me? Why I've got more out of it than all of you together."

Out at Rowan Farm the days to Whitsun were being counted. There were so many things Margret and Matthias had to show Andrea, Joey and Mother. Besides the young lambs and pups, there was Betsy's pretty calf, a heifer, glistening brown with a pink nose and large, velvety-black startled eyes. Laura's chicks, too, would have to be shown, and the yellow balls of fluff that were the young ducks. The turkey-hen who had hatched them out and considered herself their mother kept leading them toward the edge of the woods, and everyday they escaped from her and made for the little pond. And then there were Marri's bees to see and her two goats and Rowan Farm's fields and gardens and woods in their spring glory, and the stream in the valley which now looked so peaceful, though during the spring thaws it had roared and plunged and flooded the meadows and fields down below.

It was lucky that Margret and Matthias had so much work from morning till night. At least time did not drag.

CHAPTER ELEVEN

A Happy Whitsun Visit

AT LAST the Friday before Whitsun arrived and Matthias drove in to bring the family back from town.

"You can't do a lick of work today," Kathrin scolded Margret, who would drop her potato-peeling every five minutes to run to the gate and listen for the pounding of hoofs and the rattle of wheels.

First thing in the morning they had gone to the woods to pick young birch branches, and to Mrs. Almut's garden for daffodils and tulips, and had made bouquets to decorate the rooms of Noah's Ark. How pretty the four beds with their checked spreads looked in the bright light of a May morning. In front of the coffer bench by the window stood the old table, covered by a clean tablecloth. Through the windows a patch of forest with dark firs and light birches could be seen. Next to this was the big sheepfold. The section fenced off for the lambs ran close up to the Ark. The lambs had to be separated from their mothers for a while now, so that they could be weaned. Mornings Margret had only to

open the door and call, "Rachel!" and a fleecy little white
thing came rushing up, actually climbed the steps and
pushed its nose into the Ark, although its manners were still
none the best. Lumpi, too, sometimes paid a visit to the Ark.
He had discovered that he needed only to leap over the haw-
thorn hedge, and he did so whenever he felt that Margret
had been neglecting him.

The elderberry bushes near the Ark were already in full
leaf. All the greenery roundabout was becoming to the old
railroad car, softening its harsh lines and making it look like
a long low cottage. Farther off, on the edge of the woods, a
larch was in flower, its tiny pink cones sending out an almost
intoxicating fragrance. The air was abuzz with bees and the
pastures were golden with dandelions. The cherries and
plum trees were done blooming; but the apples were wearing their pink Whitsun dresses, and underneath them the
cows moved slowly along, dipping their wet noses into the
golden stars, chewing contentedly and occasionally mooing
to express their happiness.

How long it was since Margret had experienced a spring.
She counted back. Last year she had been moving about.
That spring had been spent in filthy railroad cars and ugly
barracks, a spring without home or hope, so that all the
brightness only made her life seem more gloomy. And
two years ago? By then her child's world had already
been shattered, their home broken up, Father away and
Christian and Cosi dead. The old apple tree by the wall had
just started flowering when Mother and Matthias had dug
the grave underneath its branches. Margret had not helped;
she had been as if dead herself, so numbed by what had happened. Even now she would have recurrences of that feeling,

and she would feel a sudden terror of darkness and intense anxiety when the barking of a dog woke her from sleep at night. But out here in the country everything had changed; all the hard knots inside her had somehow loosened.

When the cart finally turned into the lane, Margret was standing at the wide-open gate waving, while Alf and Fury raced toward the ponies, barking joyfully. Mrs. Almut came out to greet her guests. Joey was allowed to unhitch the horses and then ride to the pasture on Tony's back. No sooner had he jumped off than both the horses lay down in the high juicy grass and rolled back and forth like young fillies. You could see they were glad to be back in their meadow, away from the dust and hard pavements of the town.

Margret took her mother and Andrea by the arm and led them toward the oblong structure over whose door now hung the big, bright sign reading, "Noah's Ark."

Andrea was wild with joy at this fulfillment of her dream. "Oh, Mummy, they've really done it," she cried. "Look at the beds, two tiers, just like on a real ship. That's the way Noah must have had it in his Ark. I want to sleep on top, Margret, can I? And what a nice chest—is that for animals or people? And even a stove for the winter. Where does Matthias sleep?"

She did not wait for answers; she had already flitted through the Ark and discovered the room where Joey was going to sleep with his big brother. Then she ran out to greet Rachel, reappeared and declared, "Tomorrow we'll play Noah's Ark. We'll play with real live animals."

"Yes, we'll take them all into the Ark and you can clean

up afterwards," Margret said laughingly. "No, we don't need to play Noah's Ark. I have all I want of the Ark from morning till night. But if you like you can get up at six with me tomorrow morning and make the rounds of the animals."

That was something to look forward to—only Andrea could not wait that long. She had to run out to Lumpi at once. He was standing along the hedge, waiting for someone to pay attention to him. Then she stuck her nose into the empty horse stable and looked into the cowbarn, where there was only one lonely calf in his stall.

Meanwhile Margret had noticed, with alarm, how pale and tired her mother looked. "What have you done to yourself, Mummy?" she asked with concern, while her mother sat down on the bench by the window and looked out happily at all the fresh greenness of the outdoors. It was so wonderfully soothing after the cramped house on Parsley Street and the grey city full of rubble. "You've been overdoing it, sewing for the boys, Mummy, haven't you? They tear their things as soon as you've mended them. You must really rest up here. I'll be very quiet tomorrow when I get up, so that you won't wake. And after chores I'll come in for breakfast. Mrs. Almut says we can all have our breakfast together here during the holiday."

"When do you get up?"

"At six, just the same as in winter, but now it's really four because of this silly double daylight saving time. First the cows have to be milked so that Mrs. Almut can deliver the milk. Then the sheep. We keep all the sheep milk for ourselves, and we churn butter from the cream twice a week. You know, I had to learn to milk all over again when I started on them. They have such firm, round udders, altogether different from the cows. But since I've started singing to the animals while milking I don't have any trouble. I even get foam on top of the milk."

Matthias came in and sat down beside his mother on the coffer bench. He looked strong and healthy. His hands were already deeply tanned from the bright spring sun, and his mother felt her mind greatly relieved as she studied him. In his face there was no trace of the frowning discontent that had formerly, in the city, alarmed her. She still could not see what his future would be, but for the immediate present she need not worry about him. That meant a great deal to her.

That evening when the younger children were asleep and Matthias had to go off on an errand, Mother and Margret sat and talked with Mrs. Almut for a while. The professor, too, dropped by; he was eager to meet the mother of the two young people whose lives much concerned him these days. Together they all had one of those quiet conversations which round out a good day so beautifully. Afterwards, Mrs. Lechow and Margret walked the dogs down the lane to the stone bench once more and looked out over the dark countryside which lay so peacefully beneath the starry sky.

"Well, what about you, Margret?" Mother asked, taking her daughter's hands in hers. As she did so, she felt how hard and rough those delicate child's hands had become. But this did not trouble her; she knew that calloused hands are good for getting a firm grip on life.

"What about me?" Margret repeated. "Oh, Mummy, sometimes I think I'll just fall over, I'm so tired. And yet I know I wouldn't change places with anybody in the world."

"Then it's all right," Mother said.

"Oh yes," Margret said, and she pressed her head against her mother's shoulder and breathed in happily the fresh night air, fragrant with the smells of earth and woods and plants. "Oh yes!"

Next morning Joey followed Matthias around like a dog. He went along to the barn, took up the manure fork, and was amazed to discover how hard it was to throw even half a forkful through the little door on the manure heap. He helped feed the horses and cows. Together with Matthias he visited the coldframes and the hotbeds, and then rushed out to the strawberry patch on the chance that there might be a few ripe berries. But although it was already the end of May, it would be a while before there would be any berries on these hills.

Andrea did not find it as easy as she had thought to get out of her comfortable bed at such an ungodly hour of the morning. But she would not have missed anything for the world. She stood by during the milking and sang an accompaniment to Margret's song which the cows seemed to enjoy.

Difficult old Betsy, the queen of the barn, had become gentle and sweet since the birth of her new calf, and she made it perfectly plain that from now on she wanted to be milked only by Margret. Undoubtedly this was because she was a musical cow and nobody else sang to her during the milking. If Margret ever forgot to sing, she turned her head reproachfully, rubbed her nose against Margret's sleeve and uttered an offended, "Bro-rooo."

While Margret filtered the milk she briefed Andrea on the different barn animals. Carla would soon be drying off, she told her. Jo had had a bull calf last January. Hulda was to

calve again in the winter. Mrs. Almut preferred having some
of the cows freshen in summer and others in winter, Margret said, so that they would always have a good supply of
milk. But sometimes calculations went awry.

Then Andrea had to run off to the kitchen to get hot water
from Kathrin. The water was mixed with milk which Margret fed the calf from a pail.

"Why don't you let her drink from her mother?" Andrea
asked. "It would be lots easier."

Margret, the experienced farm woman, tenderly pressed
Ute's dripping, milky snout into her apron and informed
her sister, "It's better to teach them to drink from the pail
right off. You should have seen the fuss she made at first,
snorting and puffing and butting, and I had to keep my fingers in the pail for her to suck on. But this way you know
exactly how much she's getting, and the weaning is easier
later on. Yes, there's lots you've got to know. Farming is a
science."

After the milking they went on to the hens, who were already raising a fearful cackle, impatient to get out to the
dewy meadow to find worms and fat snails. Laura led out
her chicks. She was a proud and pugnacious mother. Nobody, not even the handsome cock of the roost, could get too
close to her flock or steal a grain of corn from her chicks.
Even the big turkey with her yellow ducklings kept a respectful distance from Laura.

Andrea loved taking the big brown eggs out of the nests
and putting them into a basket. "Mummy can have one for
breakfast, Mrs. Almut said," Margret told her. "And now
you see to it that your wives lay well today," she ordered the
cock. "Kathrin wants to bake a cake; tomorrow is Whitsun-

day." The big cock with his iridescent green tailfeathers and blood-red comb shook his plumage, puffed out his chest and looked extremely conscious of his duties.

"Today the henhouse must be given a thorough cleaning," Margret said. "So that everything will look good for Whitsun. The farmers' wives are always complaining about how poorly their hens lay, but when you look at their henhouses you see the reason. What hen would want to lay eggs in such filthy nests? They have such poor grade stock running around. They don't try to propagate the best layers, and most of the time don't even know how old their hens are."

From the henhouse they went on to the sheep, which were already out, for their shed door was open day and night now and each of the different boxstalls had a separate exit to a part of the fold. Andrea wanted to hug the lambs, but they were chary of strangers. They stamped their little hoofs, threw their heads to one side and suddenly jumped into the air with all four legs stiff. Then they scurried madly away.

The mothers were milked right out in the field. Then Andrea was delegated to take the milk to Kathrin in the kitchen while Margret took care of Lumpi.

"And now for the dogs," Margret said when Andrea returned to the kitchen.

As soon as they entered the pups' nursery five whelps scrambled around their feet and Ate jumped down from her beam to greet Margret. Apparently she did not entirely approve of Andrea's visit, for she growled softly while Margret held her collar tightly. "Easy, Ate."

It was hard to avoid stepping on the pups. Each of them wanted to be petted first, and of course each wanted to get at the food first. Along the wall of the doghouse was a rack holding five small bowls, one for each of the little gluttons. Each bowl was in a separate compartment to prevent the pups from gobbling each other's portions. The rack was so made that it could be raised as the animals grew—stooping while eating might spoil the fine line of their necks. Margret explained all these details to Andrea, who was astounded. It was a satisfaction to Margret to show her sister that there were some things which could not be learned in school.

The kennel had to be thoroughly cleaned today, since it was Saturday. The pups were wonderfully helpful about the cleaning. They took turns snapping at the broom, dragging away the dustpan, hanging on to Margret's apron or playing tug-of-war with the precious dustrag.

"They can really wear you out," Margret finally admitted, "but I still think they're wonderful. And now we'd better get going if we want to feed the pigs before breakfast."

They hurried over to the house, where Kathrin had boiled and mashed potatoes for Sabine, the big mother sow. Skim milk was sloshed over the potatoes and some groats and calcium added; then the girls carried the heavy pail between them to the pigpen. What a sight awaited them there—Andrea was almost beside herself with delight. There lay Sabine, a fat, lazy mountain of ham, and like beads on a chain nine pink piglets clung to her belly, sucking greedily. But when Margret approached the trough, Sabine's maternal patience gave out. Grunting, the huge beast rolled to her feet, leaving her babies to complain in squeaky voices. She wanted her breakfast, that was all there was to it. Margret poured the feed into the trough and said a few friendly words to Sabine. But Andrea had the impression that this stately queen-mother was treated rather casually.

"Well, you see," Margret explained, "it doesn't do to get too friendly with the pigs here. Because then everybody feels bad when they have to be slaughtered. Anyway I've told Mrs. Almut that I'm going away on slaughtering day and I won't come back until they start making sausages—because that's a lot of work, so everybody has to help, of course. Sabine will be around for a long time, because she's a first-class brood sow with a pedigree like a thoroughbred horse's. The sucklings will be sold—lots of people are asking for them already. We'll be keeping only three of them to fatten. Time was the farmers wouldn't buy any of Mrs. Almut's registered stock because they were more expensive than the grade stuff. But now all the farmers have money and they want to buy the best and dearest."

Andrea nodded, much impressed. It was amazing how much her big sister knew.

The sun had risen over the edge of the woods by the time the sisters crossed the yard and returned to the Ark. On the bench under the linden sapling sat the grey barn cat, cleaning herself for the holiday. Margret petted her as she passed, and the cat poked at her hand with sheathed claws; she wanted to play. "Don't the dogs bother her?" Andrea asked.

"We never set our dogs on cats," Margret answered. "And our cat has never had to run away from dogs. I wouldn't be surprised if the enmity between cats and dogs weren't something people started."

When they came into the Ark they found that Mother was already up and had made the beds.

"You ought to be breakfasting in bed," Margret reproached her.

"The sun was so tempting," Mother said. "It would be a

shame to miss a minute outdoors. As for breakfasting in bed, do you want me to feel like a grand duchess? That's one thing I never wanted to be."

"What did you want to be?" Andrea asked.

Mother thought it over a bit, and then she said, "You know, when I think about it, I've never really wanted to be anything but the wife of a certain doctor named Andreas Lechow and the mother of his children."

On the table stood five bowls. The girls set the table with the big jug of sheep milk and a large loaf of brown, fragrant, homemade bread in the center. In a few minutes Matthias and Joey came in, and Joey had to tell about the amount of work he had already done this morning. Andrea, too, indicated that she had been slaving. At any rate, everyone was starving hungry. Margret cut thick slices of bread which were broken into the fresh, creamy sheep milk. A spoonful of brown molasses was added for sweetening, and then for a while nothing was heard but the rattling of spoons.

Mother looked happily around the circle. It made her glad to have all her four together again. "I feel as rested as if I'd spent two weeks at a resort," she said. "Later I'm going to ask Mrs. Almut whether she has anything she'd like me to sew."

"That's just like you!" the children cried in chorus. And Margret added, "Luckily Mrs. Almut won't let you do anything of the sort. You're going to have a deck chair out on the lawn and we won't let you stir until lunchtime."

They were all very stern with Mother, especially Matthias, who was already sixteen and so big and strong he could easily have lifted his mother and carried her.

"And you, Andrea, can sweep the Ark," Margret said.

"Get Alf and Fury in here to play with you and you can pretend you're Mrs. Noah. And then go to the kitchen and help Kathrin peel potatoes, and do Mrs. Almut's room. I have to hurry over to the chicken yard, and there's lots of other work for me. But if you take over some of it, I'll be through by noon and after the lunch dishes are done I'll be free until the evening milking. Then we can take the dogs for a walk across the fields to Dietholz and back through the woods."

On their way back from their walk that afternoon they came to a place where the woods thinned out. There was a narrow meadow, a small field and a tiny house surrounded by a garden. "This is the limit of the Dietholz community forest," Margret said. "And beyond that meadow Mrs. Almut's woods begin. We're going to visit Marri, whom the village children call the bee witch."

"Is she really a witch?" Joey asked.

"As far as I'm concerned she's a good fairy," Margret said. "Anyway, she is good to all animals, but people don't want to be good to her."

The garden was laid out in neat beds filled with vegetable seedlings, strawberry plants and berry bushes. Several small apple trees were in flower, and all around the house was a riot of fragrant flowers. A small rockery was a foam of rosy saxifrage and moss pink, white arabis and golden alyssum. Wild blue mountain asters swayed on slender stems, and close up to the house the visitors saw the bee house, the entrances painted in different colors, and in and out of the small holes streamed the bees, filling the air with their soft buzzing.

Joey felt a little queer when he found himself right in

front of the witch's house, just as in *Hansel and Gretel*. He reached up for Margret's hand and clung tightly to it; after all, you could never know. And then a little old woman came out of the bee house. She had a pipe in her mouth— she must be a witch, for who ever heard of a woman smoking a pipe? A cloud of smoke hovered around her like a gauze veil, and several bees were sitting in her hair. As she stepped toward them a black nanny goat suddenly peered around the side of the house, to which it was attached by a chain. Its bleating sounded like a goblin's laugh, and its slanty eyes sparkled quite green in the sunlight.

But old Marri did not look unfriendly, and as soon as she came within reach she shook hands with Margret.

"So ye're payin' a visit on old Marri, are you, girl?" she said. "Glad to see you."

"This is Andrea," Margret said. "And this is Joey. My brother and sister. They've come to the farm for the holidays."

"And you've come to call on me the very first day!" Marri said in astonishment, and Margret could see she was pleased. It was easy to hurt people unintentionally, but sometimes it was also easy to make them very happy without trying to.

"Well, it'll be midsummer before you know it," Marri rambled. "That's the best time for gathering herbs. I told you about St. John's wort for cattle. Didn't it do them good, just like I said?"

Margret nodded eagerly. Andrea stood as if spellbound; Joey had his mouth wide open.

"I'll show you what the wild orchid plant looks like, too. That takes away all sorrow, makes people forget. Would you like that?"

"Oh no," Margret said. "Not to forget. Just to remember differently."

Marri nodded her head several times. "That's well, child. There's some as wants to forget and some as wants to remember. Remembering is better, but it takes a strong heart. Remembering is good, and peace is best. A packet of fern seed under your pillow at night brings peace and puts hate away."

"Peace, yes," Margret murmured, so low that only the old woman heard her. "And put away hatred and revenge too —oh yes."

The bees hummed. A grey cat came out of the house and rubbed against Marri's legs.

"Listen to the way the woodpecker is hammering," she said, holding her hand to her ear. "Knock-knock. He's knocking at the door. Someone will be coming home soon."

"Father!" Andrea whispered. "Does she mean that Father is coming?"

"I'll give you some lavender, you black firebird. Lavender is good against will-o'-the-wisps and the little people, remember that. Did I say your father is coming? How should I know? I just heard the woodpecker knocking the way he does when somebody is coming home."

She stood still for a moment as if listening, her finger raised, and the children listened too. Knock-knock, came the sound of the woodpecker. Knock-knock-knock.

"Many never come home," the woman said. Then she laid her hand on Joey's head, and Joey looked up fascinated into her large, dark, sorrowful eyes, and he forgot that he had been afraid of her only a moment before. "Such a little fellow," she murmured. "It was only yesterday that my Ludwig looked just like him. Just a little fellow, and sweet-natured, wouldn't hurt a fly . . . What shall we give you? How about snapdragon. Put that in your pocket and you'll never come to harm."

Then she turned quickly and went into the house. When she came out again she was holding a jar of golden-brown honey in her hand. "Take that for your mother," she said to Margret. "And bring the children to see me again before they go away. I'll show you all the queen bee. I wouldn't show her to anybody else."

The children walked silently back through the woods, and though nothing had been agreed among them, none of them said a word at home about the woodpecker. But that night, before he fell asleep, Joey whispered over and over, "Knock, knock. Knock, knock, knock." Very quietly he knocked against the wooden wall of the Ark, so softly that no one heard. And then, half asleep, he murmured, "Snap-dragon so you'll never come to harm." In his sleep the big queen bee buzzed mysteriously back and forth, a huge snap-dragon opened like a golden gate, and the queen slipped in-side it. Immediately the flower rose up with her like an airplane taking off for the stars, and the stars were nothing but buzzing, singing bees. "Knock, knock," the woodpecker hammered, and Joey in his dream calling out longingly, "Come in, come in."

CHAPTER TWELVE

Death Knocks

SUMMER HAD COME, a dry hot summer that brought little rain to the usually rainy mountain foothills in which Rowan Farm lay. All day long the sun beat down upon the slope with its rows of strawberry beds, upon the raspberry patch and the field of currant and gooseberry bushes. The strawberries were already ripe, and in the noonday warmth they gave off a fragrance like sweet wine. There were strawberries and milk for supper every evening on Rowan Farm— a wonderful treat after a day's labor in the hot sun.

Every day, when Margret and Matthias spent their two hours crouching in the rows of strawberries, picking the berries for sale, a small percentage of the red fruits would vanish into their mouths. Mrs. Almut had a saying, "You must not bind the mouth of the ox who treads the grain." And Matthias and Margret were perfectly willing to work like oxen so long as they could get such sweet feed.

Almost every day visitors from the city were struck with the desire to pay a visit to their dear friend Mrs. Almut.

Over the winter she was apt to forget how many good friends she had, but when summer came they would always turn up in droves. Naturally the slaughterhouse inspector who supplied the kennel with meat all through the year had to be sent a crate of strawberries, and later raspberries and currants, and still later plums and apples. Shoemakers and saddlers and implement dealers could not go away empty-handed.

"The whole year's debts fall due when the fruit ripens," Mrs. Almut said.

Kathrin stood by the stove all day and put up preserves, and the work did not improve her temper. Almost every evening Margret had to help her pick over the berries until Mrs. Almut said, "Let the child go to bed, Kathrin; she needs more sleep than we do."

The first cutting of hay was already over. Those had been strenuous days for the children, since the normal work had to go on at the same time. The hot sun had given Matthias still more freckles, and his back and shoulders were perpetually beet-red. Margret's whole skin turned golden bronze. From all the sun her hair took on a coppery gleam, and her lips were as dark-red as the ripe berries she loved to eat.

The first hay crop was a good one, but it looked like a dry summer and Mrs. Almut said they must start conserving feed early. So the sheep were allowed to run among the young fruit trees and graze off the thistles and witch-grass before Matthias went through the fields with the toothed harrow. Someone had to be herdsman to the sheep to keep them from getting into the berry bushes. Sometimes, too, they were staked out near the edge of the woods. They were not very happy about this, but if they had been allowed to roam freely they would soon have moved over into the garden or the horse pasture, where the grass was closer and juicier. Emil the ram was especially offended by this loss of freedom. He pawed and stamped and ran around and around his stake, bleating loudly, until his long chain was all wound up.

"It's the same way every year," Mrs. Almut said. "The first few days they complain and are offended, but they get used to it after a while and eat nicely. Then, when they go back into their fold in October again, there's a good second growth and they find enough to keep them busy until snow falls. The rule is that seven months out of the year sheep do with feed that wouldn't keep a cow. Otherwise it doesn't pay to raise them."

Since the pasture was pretty well grazed down and the clover still had to be reserved, the cows were taken out every evening and walked along the broad strips of grass dividing the fields, or by the edge of the woods, for an hour or more. Margret would take two of them at a time on a chain and walk gently along by the grassy banks of the brook, where there were always spicy weeds and fresh grass. She carried a leafy branch in her hand to ward off flies. Her main concern was that neither of the cows should get away and go over into the beet field, the oats or the clover. Sometimes little Rachel ran along with them; she was always demanding and getting special privileges. It was hard to resist her because she was affectionate and as obedient as a dog, and would have liked best following Margret around all the time. Margret loved these quiet grazing hours in the evening when she had time to think over all the day's doings.

The pups were growing rapidly and giving her more pleasure every day. But one day, when Mrs. Almut and Margret happened to be together in the kennel, the American captain appeared again. He had brought a friend with him, and they wanted to buy two of the pups. The jeep stopped out on the road and the two men came through the gate into the yard. The dog he had bought came with them. Barking with joy, Arjopa leaped up at Mrs. Almut as she came forward from the kennel to greet the guests. Arjopa was huge, somewhat bigger than Alf, and the captain was terribly proud of himself for having selected the best dog. As far as he was concerned, the superiority of a Great Dane was measured by its size.

Margret looked critically at the dog. Arjopa really was handsome, and was obviously getting a wonderful diet. "Come here, Arjopa," she said, taking the dog's head between her hands. "Your forehead might slope a bit better," she said to it. "And that back paw of yours. . . . Oh well, the main thing is that your master thinks you're the finest dog in the world."

This time the Americans wanted a male and a female. But Mrs. Almut had so many requests from breeders that she was not very eager to sell her dogs to the two officers, who were only ordinary dog-lovers, after all, not professional breeders.

Margret had to do the interpreting—and she was grateful for how well her father and mother had taught her English. She leaned against the kennel fence in the leather shorts that had once belonged to Mrs. Almut's son, a knot of pups scrambling around her long tanned legs, her clear grey eyes turning from Mrs. Almut to the young soldiers and back again. Coolly, distinctly and in good English she asked and answered the questions from all sides.

So Mrs. Almut only wanted to sell one dog? the Americans asked. Oh, that was too bad. They'd promised a friend they'd bring back a young female for him; he was going home soon and had got it into his head that he wanted to raise Great Danes on his father's farm. They really liked that light-colored little female. And Mrs. Almut ought to take into consideration how well the dogs would be fed back in the U.S.A.

"Are you actually planning to take the dogs back home with you when you return to America?" Margret asked this on her own responsibility.

"Of course we are," the captain assured her. They would never part with their dogs, he said.

"You really mean it?"

"We really mean it."

"Because you see we don't like the dogs passing from hand to hand. I've heard that you Americans usually resell them. You just want them for a pet for the time you're here."

It was almost a cross-questioning. Margret gave the two soldiers a stern, searching look, as though considering whether they could really be trusted.

"On my word of honor," the captain said, and he smiled at her like an overgrown boy promising not to be naughty. This young lady with the funny leather pants and short-cut hair was certainly a tough customer. Still, you had to grant that she looked just as much of a thoroughbred as the dogs. The captain's handsome, carefree face turned suddenly pensive. What could this child expect to get out of life in her impoverished, wrecked country? It was certainly hard luck being a German girl in these times. But she looked as though she'd make her way somehow or other.

"You understand we don't want the whole price in money," Margret said, after Mrs. Almut had stated the sum.

"Okay," the captain said. "Sure."

"Some coffee, chocolate and tobacco. The tobacco is for our men," Margret added hastily. She saw that the two of them were beginning to smile at her again. It really was sort of silly, the way she had said "our men." She began blushing —which made her feel still worse. But her tone was sterner than ever.

"Okay," the captain said again, and made an effort to look serious and respectful.

"You can come and get the dogs in a month. Their ears have just been clipped and will have to heal."

They agreed to take Birch and Bayard. Then they lured Arjopa back into the jeep and roared off, waving gaily back to the inhabitants of Rowan Farm.

"You handled that beautifully, Margret," Mrs. Almut said, laughing. "So, we'll have coffee for breakfast for a while longer."

The following Friday, when she drove into the city again, Margret took along a basket of strawberries for Mother and a smaller basket for Mrs. Verduz. Matthias took the opportunity to drive quickly over to Dieter's to ask whether he'd be able to come out again to help with the building of the Ark.

With one lithe leap Caliph sprang to Margret's shoulder as she entered Mrs. Verduz's kitchen.

"Good morning," Margret said. "This is a basket of straw-berries from Mrs. Almut."

"For me!" Mrs. Verduz exclaimed, while Margret mur-mured endearments to Caliph. In town strawberries were not to be had for love or money. "Really for me?" she asked again, as though she could not believe it. "But Margret, my dear, what can I possibly give Mrs. Almut in return? I haven't anything to exchange."

"No need of that," Margret reassured her. "They just cost the regular price, two marks a pound."

"I really don't know whether I should," Mrs. Verduz said, gazing at the strawberries as though they were a miracle. "But I can't resist them." Such wonderful strawberries being offered her for mere money—and not even at the Black Market price. It was beyond belief.

"And how are you otherwise, Mrs. Verduz?" Margret asked sympathetically. "Have your headaches let up now that the house is quieter?"

"What a thing to say! None of you have ever bothered me, not for a minute. But I've had so many troubles lately I'm just sick and worn out. Those people from the Housing Office wanted to take away my parlor and move another family in, and turn the laundry into a kitchen for them. What do you think of that?"

"You really hardly ever use the parlor, Mrs. Verduz. And just think what such a fine room would mean to a refugee family."

"Oh, Margret, what are you saying?" Mrs. Verduz moaned, and she began to cry. "The doctor has given me strict orders not to have any kind of excitement—it might be the death of me, he says. But you know what I'm doing now? I'm willing my house to the city on condition that they will at least let me die here in peace. My relatives in Burghausen don't need it, they have no children, and my niece in America will certainly never need it. I've just been drawing up my will and I'm going to the notary with it so that everything will be straightened out. Then at least they'll let me alone. Tell me if there are any of my things you'd like, Margret; I want to leave you a little present too."

"Caliph," Margret said.

"Well, my dear, he's yours when I have to go beyond. But I count on living a good many years yet, let me tell you that. If only to spite the Housing Office. I'll live till at least ninety —my grandfather lived to ninety, too."

As Margret went upstairs, she heard her mother's sewing machine humming.

"Oh, Mummy, we'll have to chain you to our easy chair," she said as she kissed her mother. "You'll sew until you're all bent and crooked."

Proudly, she showed her mother the fine strawberries and relayed an invitation from Mrs. Almut to come out on Sunday with the children, in time to pick raspberries and the first currants. And Mrs. Almut wanted to know whether she could not come out during the summer holidays and do a couple of hours' sewing for her every day. Mrs. Almut also knew of a neighboring farm whose owner would be happy to have her and the children stay for a week, in exchange for sewing, if such an arrangement would be agreeable to her.

"My first country clients," Mother said. "But I can't stay away from Mrs. Verduz for any length of time. I was really

worried about her just recently; she had a severe heart attack
and the doctor had to be called."

"Yes, I know, on account of the wicked Housing Office. And how is our fairy prince, Hans Ulrich, coming
along?"

"Oh, the fairy prince!" Mother said, sighing. "Would you
believe that the boy looks thinner than he used to? The
Hertrichs are keeping him permanently and are completely
devoted to him. They want to adopt him. A few days ago I
had a long talk with Mrs. Hertrich. She's terribly worried
because the boy is so pale and quiet and won't eat properly.
Can you imagine that—Hans Ulrich who never left a crumb
on his plate?"

"It's not too surprising," Margret said. "Remember what
a big change all this is for him. He's probably a little depressed by all this luxury—he used to enjoy his harum-
scarum life so much."

In honor of her trip to town Margret was wearing a simple
dress instead of her leather shorts. The dress had once belonged to Mrs. Almut, but she was so much shorter than
Margret that a flounce had had to be added to the hem. Since
sewing had never been one of Margret's strong points, the
flounce had turned out rather too wide and the long dress
made her look almost grown-up.

"How pretty you look," Mother said, studying her big
daughter with satisfaction.

"Pretty?" Margret exclaimed in genuine amazement. "I
wish I were wearing pants. Skirts get in the way of your
legs."

Downstairs they heard the cart drive up. The horses were
left in charge of one of the neighbor boys and Matthias, who

had picked up Joey on his way home from school, came up-stairs with him.

"Hurray, strawberries," Joey shouted. Margret took hold of a tuft of his blond hair and asked, "How do you like the Quaker school lunches, squirt?"

"Marvelous," Joey said. "Sometimes I can't eat it all and then I bring some home to Mummy."

"Yes," Mother said, "and Andrea does the same. The chil-dren keep me fed."

"That's lucky," Matthias said. "Otherwise there'd be noth-ing left of you, you poor normal consumer. It's awful how thin you are."

"That's just my build," Mother said, looking uncomfort-able as she always did when she was being talked about. "I never did put on any weight."

Mother unfortunately belonged to the group called "nor-mal consumers," like all housewives. For housework from morning to night, sweeping and scrubbing floors, carrying wood, lighting fires, shopping and standing in lines, cooking and washing dishes, darning and mending, washing and ironing—this officially wasn't considered hard work.

When Margret and Matthias came back to Rowan Farm, they found the place in a state of great excitement. Joseph was going around growling and puffing dark clouds of smoke from his pipe—the tobacco was of his own raising. "Those people ought to be put behind bars," he grumbled. "Taking the farmer's last cow away and afterwards they wonder why they can't get any milk."

Kathrin was standing at the door, wailing. "Three cows is all they want to leave us. Three cows when we used to have six standing in the barn. Where are we going to get manure for top-dressing the fields?"

"What's happened?" Margret asked.

"Oh, the Commission was here," Joseph said. "They're confiscating cattle all over the country. We had to give 'em a cow and a sheep."

Margret listened in silence. She always suffered when any of the farm animals had to leave, especially when it was for slaughter. All the young pigs except three were already gone. In a month the captain would be coming for the dogs. There were only three lambs left—the number of their animals was shrinking all the time. But as soon as she recovered from the first shock she remembered the sunken-faced city dwellers and said, "There really is a reason for it, though. The people in town are starving."

Mrs. Almut came out of the house and asked, "What do you think about it, children?" She was calm, as always; she was one of those rare persons who can be detached about their own affairs.

As he unhitched the ponies, Matthias said, "Margret has a point there; the people in town are hungry."

"I know," Mrs. Almut said. "It's lucky we have the calf to raise, and who knows, we may be short of feed in the winter. But I'll find it hard to give up our beautiful Jo. And they want to take Jonathan, too, Margret."

Jonathan was the young ram. The Commission had really wanted big Emil, but Mrs. Almut had made them see that the ram was necessary for breeding purposes, not only for herself but for all the farmers roundabout who had been buying lambs from her in recent years.

Depressed, Margret changed her clothes in the Ark and

then went to the dogs' kitchen to prepare their meat. Ate
was living in the Ark all the time now and would let no one
come in when Margret was away except Mrs. Almut and
Matthias. The pups were alone in the kennel. Margret called
to them as she crossed the yard with their bowls. Ordinarily
they would be standing at the fence waiting for her. But today only Bayard and Birch came trotting slowly up in
answer to her call, and even when she reached the kennel
gate none of the others stirred. She looked into the little
shed. There lay the three others on their sides, gasping
softly. They greeted her with a feeble wagging of their tails.
Cold with fright, Margret knelt down beside them in the
straw and looked them over. They had hot, dry noses and
clouded eyes. The sickness could not have come from the
clipping of their ears, for the ears were long since healed.
Margret realized at once that it must be distemper, and she
knew what that meant. Once she had lost a whole litter of
Cosi's to that terrible disease.

The days that followed were ghastly. The veterinarian
lived far away, and when he came, hours after being called,
he had no distemper serum. "What can we do when the most
essential medicines aren't to be had?" he said wearily. "I
don't even have gasoline to get around to all my calls." He
gave them instructions and promised to look in again in two
days. Luckily Mrs. Almut still had a stock of animal medicines, and a rich experience in using them. Margret arranged
one compartment of the Ark as a sickroom and took turns
watching with Mrs. Almut. They did not leave the animals
alone at any time of the day or night. Together they fought
the vicious disease, and whenever Margret was on the point
of losing heart she had only to look into Mrs. Almut's un-

daunted eyes. "Don't be afraid," Mrs. Almut said. "Fear never helped anything."

Soon all five dogs were lying on their sides, breathing shallowly, nose and eyes dripping, coughing harshly and painfully. They were given poultices for the cough, camomile steam for their clogged nasal passages, and every hour they were hand-fed hot milk with cough medicine. Mrs. Almut also had distemper pills, but these did not seem to help.

On the fourth day the vet came back. He looked grey with weariness; he had spent half the night on the road because his old motorcycle had had a flat tire. There was nothing to do about the dogs now but wait and see, he said. If Mrs. Almut had some whiskey she could give them each a spoonful in hot milk. The important thing was to keep up the pups' strength. Bayard and Bashka were already breathing a bit more freely, he thought.

During this battle with sickness, Margret did not feel much like singing while she milked, and the cow mooed discontentedly. Margret looked like a ghost when at six in the morning she arrived in the barn with her milk pails. She had dark rings under her eyes and once, when Mrs. Almut asked her, "When did you last eat a meal?" she only shrugged.

"I'd like to get Marri in to help," she said on the evening of the fifth day.

"Let's do that, Margret," Mrs. Almut said. "I've thought of that more than once. Even the farmers send for her sometimes when they don't know what to do about a sick animal. Then if she isn't able to help them, they say she bewitched their cattle."

Margret ran at top speed through the woods and knocked on the door of the little house. She poured out her story. Marri merely nodded, gathered up some bottles and little packages, and came with Margret at once. At the Ark she bent over the poor, shrunken little pups, asked a few questions, and then took out one of the bottles she had brought with her. She let a few drops of liquid trickle into each of the gaping mouths. When she straightened up, Ling was standing at the door. He was looking at Marri, as indeed all the others were, but her quiet, patient face was inscrutable. She rummaged in her large bag, took out a package of dried herbs, and sent Matthias to the kitchen to brew a tea. "Everything you've done so far is good," she said. "But we'll try something else, too." And she produced a jar of salve and a larger bottle. "It's too bad the sickness has already reached the stomach," she said. "But this may help."

"Can Ling make suggestion?" the Chinese asked modestly. Marri nodded, and everyone turned to look at Ling.

"Ling nothing know about dog," he said. "Ling only know sick people with big pain in belly. Would Mrs. Almut give Ling little bit coffee?"

Marri nodded again. She seemed to trust the Chinese.

Mrs. Almut hurried back to the house with Ling and took out her coffee canister. She held it toward him, but he said, "Not need velly much."

He picked out some twenty coffee beans and roasted them to coals on the hot stove top. Then he took a mortar from the mantelpiece and pounded the charred beans to a fine powder. They returned to the Ark and poured a little of the powder into each pup's mouth.

"One hour tea, one hour Ling's powder. All night," he

said. Then he bowed and vanished as noiselessly as he had come.

"Do as he says," Marri ordered. "And keep rubbing salve into the nose, a drop from the little bottle into the eyes, a spoonful from the big one into the mouth. I'll come again after midnight." She left.

Mrs. Almut wanted to send Margret to bed, but Margret shook her head vehemently. "All right," Mrs. Almut said, patting Margret's hair. "Then I'll lie down for a while and relieve you later on."

"I want to ask you a question," Margret said.

"Well?"

"What is the story about Marri's son?"

"Have spiteful tongues been wagging again?" Mrs. Almut said. She was silent for a while, helping Margret with the dogs. But after they finished the round of treatments, she said, "How can I explain it to you, child? I know what people say. Some say he was crazy, others that he was a coward. None of it's true. I knew Ludwig from the time he was a baby. He was just one of those people who wanted to take Christianity seriously, you understand? Love your enemies and thou shalt not kill—he took it all literally. They didn't give him much of a chance during the war. Either-or, they said. Kill or be killed."

"Oh, Lord," Margret moaned.

"That's the way it is, child. The finest porcelain is the soonest broken. And yet those are the people we need most now, in these difficult times when a new world has to be built. But Marri has got it into her head that his death was her fault. 'I should have raised him differently,' she says. 'In a world of wolves you have to learn to howl with the wolves.' "

"Poor Marri. Doesn't she realize that he was a hero, maybe a greater hero than the ones with medals?"

"That's true, Margret, and someday she'll realize it. It takes time to heal sorrow."

Then Margret was left alone with the dogs. It was fortunate that she had so much to do. As soon as she had finished one round of salving, tea, spoonfuls and coffee powder and drops from the small bottle, she could almost begin again at the beginning. The little patients were touchingly passive. But feeble as they were, each time she spoke to them they wagged their tails once or twice and looked up at her with clouded eyes. And she spoke to them often, whispering affectionate, pleading words to them. "Get well, my darlings. Please, please, get well. Take this nicely, Bashka, sweet. Come, let me give you the drops, Bayard. Yes, I know it tastes horrible, but it will do you good."

She held their heads high, poured the powder or the liquid into their mouths and then held their snouts shut in her hand so they could not spit out the medicine. They were so good and patient; even though Margret was tormenting them with this constant medication, they pressed their heads affectionately against her hand.

It had grown dark outside. The wind soughed through the trees. A night bird cried out. In the sheep shed the sheep were shifting about, and a chain rattled in the cowbarn. Once it seemed to her she heard Matthias get up and go out to the horse barn. How many noises there were on a summer night. But most of the time she listened only to her pups' harsh, painful breathing. Toward ten o'clock she thought that little Birch was becoming quieter. But Battak was breathing harder and harder, and from time to time a convulsive twitching passed through Bona's body. Shortly before eleven the little female crept closer to Margret, wearily placed its head on her knee and looked up at her with eyes full of terror and a plea for help. Margret took the dog on her lap and caressed the twitching body.

"Bona, my darling, you must hold out," she whispered. "You'll get better again. In a few days you'll all be well."

She had to talk to encourage herself. And then again came the eternal round of salve, drops, tea, coffee powder and more drops. She must not, must not think that there was no hope. As she sat there with the sick pup on her knees, she recalled all the many mothers with sick or dying children she had seen during their flight in the early months of 1945, when the endless stream of refugees had passed through her town and there had been new strangers in their house every night. She thought of those who had carried their dead children with them for miles and miles, staring with lifeless eyes, inflamed by tears, at the frozen little corpses, unwilling to part with them, until at last some merciful person gently buried them in the snow on the edge of the highway. It seemed as though all the world's suffering had come down at once upon her and was suffocating her. And she thought of Marri also, who had to suffer shame in addition to sorrow over the loss of her son.

She saw that Bona was growing quieter, and bent over the pup. It lifted its head once more to her, wagged its tail gently, and then its twitching body stretched out and grew stiff.

When Marri returned at midnight, two of the dogs, Bona

and Battak, were dead. Margret went on treating the others; she saw Marri through a mist of tears. The old woman quietly caressed the girl's shaking shoulders.

"Keep on," she said. "While there's life there's hope."

Margret cried and cried, while the old woman's calloused hand stroked her again and again until she grew calmer. She had wept out all her tears, like a spring gone dry. When Mrs. Almut returned an hour later, she was sound asleep on the bench, utterly exhausted by her sorrow. Marri had laid a burlap bag over her bare legs and gone on tending the pups.

"We'll pull these three through," she said.

Margret awoke at her usual time and went across to the barn. Leaning her head against the cows' sides, she fell asleep again several times while milking, and would start awake when the cow mooed in astonishment. She poured the milk through the filter into the big milk cans and called Matthias, who always helped her to lift the heavy cans into the wagon.

Matthias said nothing to her, but he kept looking at her while they took care of the milk cans. When they were finished, he gestured with his head toward the horse barn. "Quiet," he said at the door, "she's still a little excitable."

Mimi was standing in her box, rolling her eyes and twitching her ears restlessly. The other pony had thrust her head over the partition between them and was looking down into her stall.

"Easy, Mimi," Matthias said. "Easy, old girl."

They went into the stall, and Matthias placed his arm carefully around the mare's neck. She whinnied, a low, proud cry. There was something lying on the floor beside her. She bent her head down as if to show it to them. It moved, raised a small nose toward its mother, and tried to get up on its pipestem legs, which were so absurdly long. Suddenly it was standing, swaying, looking at them with large, moist, timid eyes—the most perfect little creature imaginable, alive from its tiny hoofs to the rosy, softly quivering nostrils. The mother bent her long neck over the colt and ran her tongue over the stiff, woolly mane.

"Life!" Margret thought. It was too much for her; it overpowered her, and suddenly she found herself leaning against the wall of the box, and everything looked foggy. Matthias slapped her on the back encouragingly. "Well," he said, "well, Margret, old battle-ax."

"Yes, yes, I'm all right," Margret said, dabbing her eyes with her stable apron because she had no handkerchief. "It's only—only because it's so beautiful, Matthias."

Slowly the wasted bodies of the three pups gathered strength, and slowly Margret's pale cheeks regained their color. But this new experience with death had opened her old wound, and she kept thinking about Christian and Cosi. She also thought a great deal about Marri during the next few weeks, and her own sorrow calmed as she compared it with the hopeless loneliness of the old woman.

One evening she was again pasturing the cows along the strip of grass that ran beside the road. Several children passed on their way to Dietholz. A refugee woman was picking up brushwood in the Hellborn forest. A man came down the road and stopped in front of her. He was wearing a tattered and faded coat. His only baggage was a market basket. His grey, exhausted face was half hidden by a shaggy beard.

"Well, that's Homann's Betsy," he said. "Don't you remem-

ber me, Betsy?" The big cow disregarded him; she seemed
more interested in her grazing.

"And who are you?" the man said. "I suppose you're
working on Rowan Farm. How are things there?"

"All right," Margret answered shortly, staring at the
stranger. He looked as if he had arisen from the grave and
he spoke in an oddly rough way, as if his voice were rusted
from long disuse. But he had kind eyes, kind, weary blue
eyes underneath his unkempt hair, which looked as though
it had been powdered with ashes. As she looked at him he
smiled faintly and said, "I do think you're wearing my
leather shorts."

"Yes . . . then you must be Mr. Almut."

"That's right. Call me Bernd—I can't even remember the
last time anyone called me Mister. Yes, I was once Bernd
Almut. Maybe I'll learn how to be him again. Now go on,
run along to my mother and tell her there's somebody here
who wants to see her. Be careful how you say it, I don't want
it to be too big a shock to her."

"Here, take the cows," Margret cried out, putting the
chain into his hand. "Follow after me slow and I'll run
ahead. By the time you reach the gate I'll have told her."

She flew through the yard on her long legs, while the man
followed behind, leading the two cows. "What a lovely
young girl," he thought. "To think such things still exist."

Margret had already reached the yard. "Mrs. Almut," she
called, and held her hand to her heart because it was beating
so rapidly from running and from joy. "Mrs. Almut, quick."
She saw Mrs. Almut come quickly out of the horse barn and
suddenly stand still. Her hand flew to her throat as if she
could not breathe.

"Yes," Margret called out, looking at her with radiant face.

"Margret," Mrs. Almut said, her hand still fumbling at her collar. "Where . . . where is he?"

"Knock, knock, knock." The sound came from the gate, which Margret had let slam shut behind her in her haste. "There!" she said, pointing to the gate. "I'll go back and take the cows from him."

CHAPTER THIRTEEN

Building the Ark

THE BLOSSOMS of the linden tree by the well at Rowan Farm had fallen. The summer solstice was past and the last of the gooseberries and currants tasted sweeter than any before them, for they seemed to have absorbed all the richness of the summer's heat. The grain stood high and golden, waiting for the scythe; but it was a thin stand this year, for drought had come down hard upon a land already suffering from want.

In the gable room of Rowan Farm stood the huge, painted peasant bed that Bernd's grandmother had given him on his twelfth birthday. Now Bernd Almut lay in it once more, back from across half the world after many adventures. He lay quite still all through the long, bright summer days and through the silvery nights which were like a gentle transition between the twilight of the fading day and the dawn of the next. He heard Matthias mowing clover for the cows, and he lay and waited, wondering whether he would now be permitted to stay home, or whether he must continue his

journey still further, to a land from which there was no returning.

His mother, and the professor and Kathrin, who had both
known him since he was a baby, often sat beside him. He
spoke to no one. He was too tired even for speech. The
women thought they must feed him good and nourishing
food, so that he would regain his strength. But he turned
his head away and would not eat. And even if he took something to please his mother, his starved body could not keep
it down.

Once, when Kathrin was out, Marri came to visit him. She
sat for a long time looking at this young man who had been
her Ludwig's playmate. Then she said to Mrs. Almut: "In
the Russian camps they ate raw fish and raw roots. You must
give him raw food first. Carrot juice, berry juice, a raw egg
with wine and sugar, and later a little milk."

They tried this diet, and the patient obediently took a few
sips at a time of the liquid foods he was offered.

"He's recovering," Mrs. Almut said to Margret. Even now
her indestructible optimism did not desert her. But Margret
was frightened. Who could tell whether the lure of death
would not prove more tempting than life to the sick man.

Margret came to Bernd's room now and then and watched
him as he lay there, shut up within himself, almost as distant
and strange as dying people are. Once he lay sleeping. She
stood watching him with an aching sorrow in her heart. He
had a strong and handsome face, but in the corners of his
mouth was concentrated all the bitterness of the years behind
him. Seeing this, Margret went out quietly, ashamed, as
though she had been eavesdropping on someone. He would
have to forget, she thought; otherwise he would not be able

to live. He had a great deal to forget. She waited, and one day when she was again alone with him for a while, she secretly thrust three narrow leaves with brown spots—the leaves of the wild orchid—under his pillow.

She did not know that his eyes occasionally followed her as she passed softly through his room with the timid grace of a young doe. One day he asked his mother, "Who is that girl who's wearing my shorts?"

"She's the sister of Matthias, our nursery apprentice," Mrs. Almut said, overjoyed at his showing interest at last in something. "The family is from Pomerania. Her father was a doctor; he isn't back from Russia yet."

"There were some German doctors in the camp. They helped us so much out there . . ." He made a vague gesture with his chin.

A few days later he asked, "How is the harvest?"

"Not very good. It's been too dry."

"We always used to have too much rain here."

"Yes. As a matter of fact, we're not as badly off as other places."

"Have we feed enough?"

"Just about. They've left us only three cows anyhow."

"And the potatoes?"

"The early potatoes are doing all right. The late ones must have rain."

Bernd closed his eyes again.

One day he asked to be taken out to the garden. They placed him in a garden chair under the small clump of birches. The larkspur was blooming in all shades of blue, and along the wall of the house the hollyhocks stood tall. Soon the phlox border would be in bloom. Out in the barley

field beyond the orchard the reaper was going; its humming
sounded distinctly across the fields. Sometimes the colt
whinnied and then the pup Bashka barked. She had struck
up an intimate friendship with the foal. The crickets
chirped. A butterfly settled on the sick man's thin, yellowed
hand. Now and then this hand reached into the grass beneath the low chair and plucked a few blades. Bernd studied
them with amazement, as if he had never seen anything of
the sort. Sometimes Ate came and lay down beside him. His
dangling hand lay light as a leaf upon the dog's sun-warmed
hide. It was as though he had to grope his way slowly back
to life by feeling all these living things.

Sometimes Matthias brought him a few late berries,
freshly plucked, serving them on a leaf for plate. Greenish-
yellow with silver veining, the gooseberries lay on the leaf.
The currants glistened ruby red, as if there were a tiny light
inside each berry. Bernd examined them for a long time as
though he wanted to impress their shape and color on his
memory. Then he put them into his mouth one by one and
crushed them slowly on his tongue.

The cutting of the barley was finished. The sheaves stood
in the field to dry; then they had to be taken in on the
wagon. That day Bernd got up from his chair for the first
time and walked, leaning on his stick, out to the barley field
where the men were loading the sheaves. He stood for a
while and watched. Bashka came running up and wagged
her tail cordially at him. The foal trotted curiously behind
him, its neck outstretched, its nose sniffing toward his
strange hand; then it would suddenly turn about and go
galloping off, followed by Bashka barking furiously.

The sun burned down upon bare arms and foreheads

glistening with sweat, upon a scene of liveliness and bustle. And Bernd thought: One of these days I'll be joining in. He could already feel the swing of it in his slack muscles, the movement of lifting a sheaf onto the wagon. Then he returned to his chair.

Next day, when Matthias passed him on the way to the tree nursery, Bernd called out, "How are my trees doing?"

Matthias understood the significance of that "my" as he answered, "Fine."

The American captain had meanwhile come for his dogs. It was hard for Margret to part with them, but there was no help for it. A promise was a promise. Of the five pups, Bashka alone was left, and Margret took the dog into the Ark with her. There was room enough for two in Ate's big box. After all, you couldn't leave the pup all alone in the big kennel, and anyway it was just as well to housebreak her gradually.

One day, between the barley and the rye harvest, a large truck came down the road. In it were Dieter and Hans, and they had brought with them a load of fine quality tiles, mortar, and even a bag of almost unprocurable cement. Margret opened the gate to the yard for them and called to Matthias, who came running from one of the barns.

"Tiles!" he cried out, and ran his hand lovingly over the smooth surface of the tiles. "How I need them. And cement! How do you fellows do it? How about it, can you stay here overnight?"

That was what they were going to do. In fact, they planned to stay through till Sunday. "And now let's get to work," they said, rolling up their sleeves.

They carried all the tiles into the Ark. Then they began conferring, planning and measuring. They made mysterious chalk marks all over the walls.

Margret came over from the sheepfold and looked in on them. The sight of them completely absorbed in their work worried her a little. "You really ought to ask Mrs. Almut first," she said. Whatever it was they meant to do, the railroad car was some day going to be Mrs. Almut's own house.

Mrs. Almut was just crossing the yard, and Margret called to her, "Hello, have you got a moment to spare?"

"To spare? No—but what's up?"

Matthias began explaining, with a wealth of gestures, the rather impressionistic drawings on the walls of the Ark.

"You see, it's going to be just perfect for you," he assured Mrs. Almut eagerly. "Here's where we've taken out the partition between the first two compartments. The space makes a fine bedroom. I've put in four beds there, two over two."

"Splendid," Mrs. Almut said dryly. "That's been my lifelong dream—four beds in my bedroom."

"What's that? Well, you see, if there are too many for you we can always take the top bunks out again. Next door is the little kitchen. You'll see how practical we'll make it— everything built in—just like a dining car. And the chimney will serve the big tile stove in the living room at the same time. We've got the tiles, beautiful ones, and we even have cement. All we need is an iron stove top, but we've got Hans for that."

"God help us, you monster, you can't use Hans for a stove top," Dieter put in.

"Be quiet or I'll lose the thread," Matthias said. "You see, Mrs. Almut, now we come to the best part of it. A living room made up out of three former compartments, if you please. It's sort of in a mess now, but just wait. Tomorrow we're building the stove. Then there'll be a fine bench all around it and bookcases along the walls. Here a big corner bench and table that can seat eight comfortably, and the dog's cot over here. You'll be bringing your couch over from the house anyway, won't you?"

"Why of course, so I have somewhere to sleep," Mrs. Almut said.

But Matthias was so full of enthusiasm that it just brimmed over. "He goes on and on," Margret said to Dieter in amazement.

"You see, the room takes up the whole width of the car—we've torn out all the partitions. Then on the other end of the car there's the second bedroom with four more beds—or with two, just as you like. And at both ends there's a washroom with plumbing and two closets—those aren't finished yet."

"Why, it's marvelous the way you've thought it all out, Matthias," Mrs. Almut said. "I can sleep in a different bed every night in the week."

"Just as you like," Matthias said. A strand of blond hair had fallen over his forehead; his face was flushed with excitement. "And just think that we hardly need any wood at all. We're getting almost all of it from the partitions and the seats we're taking out."

"Aside from the stuff you found in the woodshed, you robber!"

"Oh, those old boards weren't doing anybody any good."

"And as for the nails and screws from the workshop that have been saved up for years . . ."

At this point Dieter thought it time to interject a remark to relieve the tension. With his most winning smile he exclaimed, "What a wonderful household where such things as nails and screws can still be found. My compliments, ma'am."

"Nothing left of them *now,* young man," Mrs. Almut said. "You could search the whole house without finding so much as a tack."

"Oh no, there are some left," Matthias said. "There's a fine collection of nails in the cigar box in the kitchen cupboard." His eyes had an almost bloodthirsty gleam as he spoke of these.

"Good Lord!" Mrs. Almut cried out. "My last reserves."

"Don't worry, I haven't taken them yet," Matthias assured her. "Now about this matter of the owner's consent, Mrs. Almut—you don't have any objections, do you?"

Mrs. Almut sighed. "Well, if you promise me not to tear down my own house and use it for building material, go ahead. Who knows, we may need the house sooner than we think."

"After all, Bernd will probably marry soon, now that he's well."

"Of course," Mrs. Almut said, and her tanned face crinkled in a merry smile. "There's just one little detail to worry about—the girl. But you can never tell how fast such things may happen. So go ahead and build."

And she shot off across the yard because someone was calling her.

The plan for Mother and the children to come out to Rowan Farm for part of the summer vacation unhappily came to nothing. Mrs. Verduz had had several heart attacks, and Mother felt that it would not do to leave the old lady alone in the house. As it turned out, her sacrifice seemed to be in vain, for Mrs. Verduz was perfectly all right all through the school vacation.

But although Mother's not coming was a great disappointment to Margret and Matthias, they did not have much time to think about it during that summer. Throughout August all hands on the farm had turned out for the harvests, and everyone worked from morning till night. Never, it seemed to Margret, had a summer passed so quickly. Now, before she knew it, nothing but stubble was left of the grain fields. Some refugee women came out from the city and were allowed to take the gleanings. After they left Margret turned the sheep into the stubble fields, and what grain remained the sheep took. The hens and ducks had already had their harvest uninvited; they walked around with glutted looks.

The swallows in the barn were preparing for their migration southward. They had already raised two broods, although it seemed to Margret that only yesterday they had begun to build their nest. Bashka was now six months old and Margret's pride and joy. To a casual observer the pup might look like an awkward adolescent with a gait like a rocking horse, preposterously big paws and a loose skin. But Margret could already see her as a future champion. Next spring, Mrs. Almut had said, she was going to start taking the dogs to shows again. This year there had simply not been time, although a good many dog shows were once more being held. But now Bernd was back and new beginnings could be made.

How different Bernd Almut looked now from the way he

had looked when he first returned. His unkempt beard had been shaved; his dark-blond hair no longer hung dusty and ashen around a haggard face. Clipped short, gleaming, lightly curled, it framed his fine, square forehead. No one asked him about his experiences, and the lines of bitterness around his mouth were gradually disappearing. Only Margret knew that it was the leaf of the wild orchid that had banished the agonized memories from his mind. But only Margret knew, too, how careful one must be with a person whose wounds were still raw.

The potato harvest came, and Dieter and the Cellar Rats came to help with it. "The gang has to be given some fresh air once in a while," Dieter said, and he introduced Margret to his boys: Anton and Franzl and Tim and Axel. They were a wild-looking bunch—that was easy to see. Only music tamed them and held them together, that and their rough, silent, intense loyalty toward Dieter. He was the only person in the wide world who knew how to make them feel that they amounted to something. They had been thieves and Black-Marketers, loafers and tricksters. Time and again they had been caught by the police and lied their way out of their predicament. Anyway they knew that the police could not do much about them. All the jails and reformatories were overcrowded; there was no room for them. Usually the police had been content to run them out of town, and then they would start all over again in a new city. They had been through that plenty of times until Dieter brought them together.

In the potato fields they threw themselves furiously into the work, and at table they attacked the heaps of new potatoes and tomatoes with equal zest. Margret had her hands full with them. They would clump into the Ark with their shoes filthy from the fields, when any well brought up person knew enough to remove his shoes at the door. They did not make their beds and never dreamed of sweeping their room. Two of them shared a bedroom with Dieter and Matthias, the other two Cellar Rats had their beds in the haymow above the sheep shed. "Don't you dare mess up my hay," Margret warned them.

In fact she had any number of criticisms to make of them; but she could not deny that she liked them anyway. Whenever she had the chance she put something extra in their way—a few plums, a glass of sheep's milk or a thick sandwich. The boys scarcely thanked her; they mumbled something inaudible which you might, if you were willing, interpret as thanks. But they would have gone through fire for Margret. To them she was a new kind of girl. The sort of girls they had met on the road were altogether different from this serious, high-minded person, so that they didn't know quite what to make of her.

After work they helped with construction on the Ark, or they took out their instruments and played. Then all the inhabitants of the house came and listened quietly. It was strange to see how the harsh, almost tough features of these boys changed while they played. The harshness dissolved and their faces took on something of the austere beauty of angels in old woodcarvings. It was as though they themselves were an instrument upon which Dieter was playing, from which he drew the magic of a melody, the infectious tempo of a dance, the impudent gaiety of a song, the gentle sorrow of a lament.

Sometimes young people from the surrounding farms and

villages gathered out in the orchard beyond the hedge of
roses and began to dance. Tired though they were from the
day's work, they threw themselves completely into the joy
of movement. They danced almost silently, their faces lifted,
bright in the twilight, and when the music stopped they
begged for more, more and more.

"You're a Pied Piper, Dieter," Margret said one evening.
"I think they'd all follow you and your Cellar Rats into the
magic mountain."

"They sure need a magic mountain, poor kids," Dieter
said. "And we're glad to be Pied Pipers and show them the
way, aren't we, fellows?" The others nodded and gave him
a look of unlimited devotion, as though they were four stray
dogs who had at last found their master.

Later the professor said to Margret, "He's more than a
Pied Piper, that young fellow. If I'm not mistaken, Dieter
has a real gift. Some day in the future, when you see how his
music moves people, remember my words."

Mrs. Almut gave the boys their wages in fine big brown
potatoes. "You've done a good job," she said. "And next
winter you can cut yourselves some wood in my woodlot if
you run short."

They left happy.

Matthias and Bernd went through the big potato field
with the digger one more time. The gleanings, they found,
amounted to a few bags more. These were divided up, one
part as a reserve of feed for the farm, one part for Mother
in town, and the rest for the refugees of Hellborn and
Dietholz.

In October, when the rowan trees hung heavy with red
clumps of berries, another letter from Andrea came for

Margret. It was a letter on which she had evidently worked hard, in view of its serious contents. She wrote:

Dear Margret, I take pen in hand to tell you of something very sad. Please do not be alarmed, but someone has died, and it was a heart attack after all. It was Mrs. Verduz. Death strikes swiftly, Schiller says, but I had no idea it could happen so swiftly, because I was talking to her just a quarter of an hour before it happened and she had just said the city councillors would turn green when they saw how long she was going to live. And thank God, Mummy happened to be with her at the time. If she isn't in Purgatory she must be in Heaven with her sainted husband, and that will make him very happy. Mummy says you should come to the funeral and make two nice wreaths of ground pine and autumn leaves and red berries, because wreaths can't be had in town; the florists won't sell you anything unless you're an old customer. Make the wreaths nice, and the funeral is on Thursday at three.

Your very sorrowful sister,
Andrea.

P.S. Remember to say a prayer for her every night, in case she is in Purgatory, but I don't think so because she was really a kind person.

CHAPTER FOURTEEN

And They All
Went in unto the Ark

EVERY EVENING before going to bed Margret made the rounds
of the barns once more. This was not in her line of duty, but
she could not rest until she had made sure that everything
was in order.

She had to stop for a few minutes' talk with the calf Ute;
otherwise it mightn't have slept well. In the pony stall Toni
stood, snorting restively. Clearly, she too would be a mother
soon. Margret took her head in her hands, pressed her face
against the soft muzzle and took a deep breath of the good
horsy smell.

The sheep lay still, peacefully chewing their cud, but
Rachel always jumped up when Margret came in, rubbed
her head against Margret's legs and begged for her custom-
ary nighttime treat, a cider apple, a carrot or a boiled potato.
She took it for granted that Margret brought her something
every night.

Lumpi's turn came last. He was usually standing; his
ears twitched and he shifted his weight restlessly when she

approached. But as soon as he heard her familiar voice he whinnied softly and was eager for their evening talk. Nowadays Margret sometimes found someone else at the horse barn when she paid these evening visits. It was Bernd Almut, who was doing his best to win the little stallion's friendship. He had gotten to the point where he could place his arm around Lumpi's neck and Lumpi was beginning to nuzzle his hair in a chummy way. But he had also started to accustom the wild young horse to work. Lumpi was hitched up every day, at first only for a short time, then for longer and longer periods. He was used to the harness now, but the idea of actually working seemed to him altogether ridiculous. Yet he behaved very nicely. "He just has a strong character," Margret said to Bernd. "Whatever he does, he does for love. You can't get anywhere with him by using force."

"Your Bashka is much the same," Bernd said. "She only obeys when she wants to."

"She does whatever I tell her," Margret said. "And isn't she a beauty?"

"She certainly is. Anyway, I care most for the animals you have to struggle with first."

Ate and Bashka always trotted patiently along on the whole evening round, but afterward they wanted to have their turn too. Unless it were raining terribly hard, there was a short walk for them every night, down the lane of rowan trees to the stone bench on the highway. They raced across the dark pastures, taking playful nips at each other's necks · as they ran, full of joy and vigor. Margret usually stood at the intersection looking out over the sleeping countryside, and all the work and movement of the day faded out into the gentle stillness of the night.

She would stand and think over the course of the year that was now approaching its end. The last of the sugar beets had been harvested and the fall planting was done. The garden beds and the unplanted fields had been turned over and left in the furrow, so that frost, snow and rain could penetrate them. The active, many-faceted life of summer was over; it had withdrawn beneath the bark of trees, into the hard core of seeds, into the roots of plants and the dark soil. Marri's bees no longer made their round of the flowers; they stayed in their hives, making a soft, monotonous hum. They did not sleep like the hedgehogs and moles, nor fly south like the swarms of migratory birds; they lived in a waking dream their still, mysterious winter life.

The human beings, too, withdrew within the house and within the shell of their own selves. After the intense activity of summer and harvest there followed the time of quiet contemplation, of gathering forces, though within it the stirrings of the next spring were already present. Once more there were rows of potted plants in the hothouses and flats full of slips and cuttings for next year. Evenings the men sat in the kitchen and wove baskets, made birch brooms and repaired their tools for spring work. Kathrin and Joseph usually went to bed early, but Bernd, Matthias and Ling often sat up late. At this time of night the taciturn men became talkative, and their talk dealt with future plans. No matter how bad things looked in the world outside, the earth and its labor would still remain to them. And since in good and bad times people always need the fruits of the earth, there was some small hope in that. They wanted to enlarge the hothouse and set out more coldframes on the south slope of the hill. They calculated and considered.

"Couldn't we drain that swampy meadow down below the woodlot?" Matthias asked one day. "Nothing but marsh grass grows there now. It would make a good place to raise medicinal plants."

"A good idea," Bernd said. "But where would we get the labor? As it is, with the plans we've got the days will have to be forty-eight hours long."

"It wouldn't be bad to get a few boys out here who'd be tramping the streets otherwise," Matthias said. "I could talk to Dieter about it."

In Mrs. Almut's room two spinning wheels hummed every evening. At one of them sat Mrs. Almut, spinning her fine, even threads; at the other Margret suffered away, getting her threads too thick or too thin, and always breaking them off.

Two nights a week the professor joined them and read to them from a new book on the stars which friends in Switzerland had sent him. For the reading the men came in from the kitchen and the dogs stretched out comfortably near the stove. During those hours of reading the world became bigger and wider for them, the horizons lifted. The reading was like seed being placed in the ground, some day, perhaps, to flower and bear fruit.

It was good being together like this. The warm, close, sheltered atmosphere of a safe home surrounded them all, and all of them knew well what great and unmerited good fortune that was in a time of universal homelessness.

"I wonder if Marri is warm enough," Margret thought, and resolved to drop by at Marri's again in the morning and find out whether Matthias and Bernd ought to chop more wood for her. She often passed by Marri's on her morning walk with the dogs, and she was always given a hearty welcome. Marri, too, was doing spinning now that it was winter; she had exchanged honey for wool, and she also spun for the farmers for wages. "Stay a little while,' she would always say to Margret, taking her hand. "You don't know how good it is having you visit."

On a cold grey day at the beginning of November Bernd Almut and Margret drove into town with the ponies.

Margret had not visited her mother for two weeks, and she was worrying about her more and more all the time. The winter was going to be frightfully hard for the people of the town. The danger of famine was more pressing than last year. At Rowan Farm they had done their best to step up deliveries of produce.

"We are still ten times better off than the city people," Mrs. Almut said. "We cannot let them go hungry."

At the last farmers' meeting there had been a fierce debate on the question. The farmers said: "Who helps *us?* We can't buy plows, we can't buy so much as a cow chain, let alone tractors. Nobody will come and work for us for paper money. If we want anything done we have to bribe people with potatoes or hams."

"If everybody thought along those lines we wouldn't get far," Mrs. Almut had said resolutely. "We must deliver our quotas or everything will go to rack and ruin, and if everybody waits until somebody else makes a start at doing what's right, the whole country will go to the dogs. You know well enough that you're living better than you used to. And you always have enough left for swapping. Hellborn's honor depends on our getting our deliveries in on time. We also have to see that our refugees right in the village have enough food and fuel."

The mayor had nodded encouragingly when she spoke, and a few of the older farmers soberly backed her up.

Margret was thinking of this as Bernd drove the ponies down the highway. They had already reached the wrecked cemeteries and the first ruins of buildings. When they came to the square with the trees, Bernd said, "You get off, Margret. I can fetch the dog meat and attend to the other errands alone. I'll be back at the corner of Parsley Street in about two hours."

Margret nodded gratefully and jumped down. "See you later, Bernd." "So long, Margret." It was wonderful having such a long visit with Mother. As Margret reached the old house on Parsley Street, the letter carrier was just coming out of the green door, so that she was able to get in without ringing.

"Hello, Mummy, it's me!" she called on the stairs. There was no sound from upstairs. She did not hear her mother moving around, nor the hum of the sewing machine. When she pushed open the door to the gable room, Caliph jumped toward her with a little mew of joy. Her mother was sitting in the corner of the sofa, something in her hand, and so pale that Margret's heart stood still.

"Mummy!" she cried as though she were trying to wake someone who had fallen asleep. "What's the matter?"

Her mother did not reply. She put out her hand and drew Margret down beside her on the sofa. Then she held out the bit of cardboard in her hand. It was a postcard, dirty, crinkled from much handling, with innumerable crossed-out addresses on the back.

A prisoner-of-war card. From Father.

The indistinct handwriting grew still more blurred as Margret's eyes filled with tears, and her heart pounded as if it were going to burst. She held Mother's icy hand tightly in hers, and then she read the message with quivering lips. "My dears, I keep trying to write to you, but I have had no answer yet. I am well and hope to see you again."

"Well!" Margret said. "He's well, Mummy, and he hopes to see us again!"

"Yes," Mother said almost inaudibly. "Thank God!"

Tears fell upon the crumpled card with its wonderful twenty-five words. "Let me see where it comes from," Margret said, and she swallowed her tears and rubbed her eyes with her fist. The date was almost obliterated, but she managed to make it out. "Dec. 2," she spelled out slowly. "Sent on my birthday, Mummy. Dec. 2, '46— Oh God, the card is almost a year old. It's a miracle that it ever arrived. Who knows how many others have been lost. But he was all right a year ago—we know that now, Mummy, don't we?"

"Perhaps he's on his way already," Mother said. "You must ask Bernd Almut right away what happens after they're released. If only he can make it. Oh, Margret, if only he can make it; he's not so young as Bernd."

"Doctors always get slightly better treatment," Margret consoled her. That was not quite true; she had heard from Bernd that the doctors worked like supermen and that they often voluntarily stayed in order to help their fellow-prisoners. But she must not say that to Mother now.

They filled out the attached answer card at once; Margret would mail it when she went out. "What will Matthias say!" she said again and again, and then she read the card once more, although she already knew it by heart. It was Father's handwriting. His hand had rested on that card. He was well. Eleven months ago he had been well and hoping to see them again. That could only mean that he hoped to be released soon. How lucky she had come today, just at this time.

It turned out that Mother had a great deal to discuss with her.

"I'll tell you everything in order," Mother said. "You know Hans Ulrich had measles. Last week I went to see him. You should have seen how he lit up when I came into the room. He's already better, and asking for Joey every day, but they can't let Joey come in contact with him yet. The Hertrichs are doing everything imaginable for him, but he can't seem to get well. He lies there in his pretty bed, so still and pale that it really wrings my heart. Mrs. Hertrich was terribly unhappy about it and said to me, 'He won't thrive with me, Mrs. Lechow. He just won't get used to me, little wild thing that he is. You must help me.' She took me to her room and we had a long talk. Then we went back to his room and I told him, 'If you eat nicely now, Hans Ulrich, when you're all better Mrs. Hertrich will send you to stay with us for a few weeks, so Joey can help you make up for all the work you've missed at school.' At that he came to life and looked first at me and then at Mrs. Hertrich and then back at me and said, 'Do you really truly mean it, or are you just kidding me?' 'But Hans Ulrich,' I said, 'have I ever tried to fool you? Of course we mean it.' Then the child began to cry and cry, he just couldn't stop, his skinny little body was shaken by sobs and he clung to my hand as though he would never let it go again. 'You see,' Mrs. Hertrich said, and she almost cried herself. I felt so sorry for her. But I'm really glad to be having the boy here, and Joey danced a war dance when he heard about it."

"You certainly have room enough," Margret said. "And you always did want a dozen children."

Mrs. Lechow went on. "Everything would be fine, but now listen to this. Last Monday Mrs. Verduz's will was opened. The city is getting her house, her relatives in the country the excess furniture, and the dear good woman left us all the things we're using, the beds and furniture and household utensils, and in addition everything she had in the attic storeroom."

"The books too? Oh, and Caliph for me?" Margret cried, hugging the cat.

"Yes, the books, too, and Caliph for you, darling. I was really happy, let me tell you, to have a few things of our own again. Our own beds and all the linen, just imagine. That was on Monday. Then on Tuesday the relatives came and looked things over. They're awfully nice people. They gave me a great many other things, more than we need, but I know so many people who'll be happy to have the things. Next week everything they've chosen is to be packed up, and I've promised to see to that. And then, while I was making plans based on all my new prosperity, a messenger came from the city on Monday morning and read me a document. It was so full of legal terms I didn't know what it was all about at first. But finally I got the drift—we have to move out of here!"

"Move out! They must be crazy."

"No, we have to get out. A private person who inherits a house can't evict his tenants, but apparently the city can. In the 'public interest,' so the summons said. I don't have to move at once—they've generously given me until December 31. And of course they'll assign me another apartment. *One* room for the three of us; that's the best they can do. I went to see it yesterday. It's in one of the old barracks on Frankfurt Street, with acres of ruins all around. Oh, Margret, you can't imagine what the place looks like—inside and out. A horde of people all hating each other because they have to live so close together. And the filth on the stairs and in the halls. And the smell of it. I suppose there's nothing to be done. Others have to live that way, so I suppose we can stand it too. But it's really horrible; it will be awful for Father when he comes home. And it isn't right for children to grow up in such an atmosphere."

Margret could not say a word; the news was so shattering she could find nothing to say. She only patted her mother's hands and gnawed her lips.

Mother saw how upset she was and put on a confident expression. "There may be a way out," she said. "Really, I have no business feeling discouraged just when we've had news from Father. Tomorrow I'll go to the Housing Office and talk with them. Maybe I can get as far as the mayor, although it's not easy to see such bigwigs. The man at the Housing Office says the city has other plans for the house. In the public interest, of course. But maybe it won't endanger the public interest if we keep our two attic rooms. I must try, at any rate."

"We have news from Father," Margret said to Bernd almost as soon as she swung up beside him on the box. She could not keep such news to herself.

"Really!" Bernd said, and then he wanted to know all about it, where from and when and what. At home, he said, they would look up the place on the map. No one else she knew was so well able to tell her what there was to fear, what to hope for. This was the first time they had had a long talk with one another. And now that the ice was broken, Margret also told him about her mother's bad luck with the apartment.

Bernd was a good listener. He listened, only rarely asking a question. It was cold, and he threw a heavy woolen blanket around his and Margret's legs. Under the blanket they were warm and comfortable.

"We've had good luck for a whole year," Margret said. "Everything has turned out much nicer and better than we ever could have imagined. And now poor Mrs. Verduz dies suddenly, and the city which is supposed to help the refugees goes ahead and evicts us."

"Have you ever heard of officials helping anybody?" Bernd asked. "A friend of mine who has his sister living here can't get a residence permit. You have to help yourself or you're done for."

When they reached Rowan Farm, Bernd went straight into the house without saying anything. Matthias began unhitching the ponies, and Margret went into the dog kitchen, put down her basket of meat and started to heat the kettle. When she came out again Matthias was leading the ponies to their stable. Margret followed him and stepped into Toni's stall with him.

"You mustn't use Toni any more," Matthias said. "She'll be foaling in a month at most. Bernd will have to hitch that lazy old Lumpi up with Mimi so he gets some work to do instead of playing the sultan all the time."

"Matthias," Margret said, leaning her face against Toni's neck. "Matthias, there's a card from Father!"

"Father!" Matthias said. He looked wide-eyed at her, and slowly ran a handful of straw down the mare's damp flanks. Both of them leaned their arms on Toni's back while the horse bent her head to her oats, Margret on one side, Matthias on the other, and Margret told her brother all the news.

That evening Mrs. Almut called Margret in earlier than usual. Fury and Alf were lying on the cot, their tails switching gently. The lamp was lit and the little stove radiated a pleasant warmth.

"Take your wheel, Margret," Mrs. Almut said. "I have something to discuss with you."

They spun together in silence for a while. Mrs. Almut seemed to be considering. At last she said, "Bernd told me your mother has to leave her apartment."

"Yes, isn't it terrible."

"Don't worry about it, child. What is Noah's Ark there for?"

"Noah's Ark?" Margret said. And then she gasped.

Mrs. Almut chuckled softly and contentedly. She looked rather like a jolly little gnome enjoying the effect of one of his friendly tricks. "Goodness, how different she is from her son," Margret thought. With her bobbed black hair, tanned oval face, firm, energetic little body, she was completely different physically from the big blond young man who was just as serious and taciturn as Matthias. But there were some features that Mrs. Almut had in common with her son— the bright, intelligent blue eyes, the clear brow and the air of honesty, the quiet radiance of reliability and kindliness.

"Noah's Ark with its eight beds!" Mrs. Almut said. "What else is an Ark for if not to go into when the water comes up to your neck? Did you think I would let your mother move into the barracks when you belong to us here?"

"Yes, but . . . what about its being your retirement home for your old age, Mrs. Almut?"

"What's this about retirement home? Why should a young woman of sixty-ish be thinking about retiring? Anyway Bernd told me today he doesn't intend to marry for a long time. He likes things just as they are, he said. But now we must ask Matthias how far along he's come with his Ark."

"He's almost finished. They haven't quite fixed the tile stove yet, but that's all. It turned out to be harder than they expected. But Dieter knows a potter whom Hans did a favor for, and the potter will come out here on Friday and bring some firebrick along too if they can fetch him in the truck."

"Splendid. And if necessary there's the old iron stove, which is as good for heating as it's ugly to look at, and that's saying a lot. So as far as I can see, there's nothing to stop us from telling the Housing Office to go jump in the lake, and get your mother and the other two out here as soon as possible."

"Mrs. Almut, Mrs. Almut!" Margret exclaimed. She could not grasp it. It was a fairy tale. Or a story from the Old Testament, as though God Himself had said, "Fear not! For behold, here is the Ark."

The spinning wheel had stood still for some time. Suddenly Margret jumped up and rushed to the door so fast that both dogs barked. She pulled open the door and called out, "Matthias?"

"Need me for anything?" Matthias answered from the kitchen.

"Yes, hurry up. Oh, you awful slowpoke. We can have Mother in the Ark with us! Isn't it wonderful. Mrs. Almut says so."

Matthias stood at the door, and his mouth slowly widened into an enormous grin from ear to ear. "Gosh," he said, "that's great of you, Mrs. Almut."

"Lucky you made all those beds," Mrs. Almut said. "But now you'll really have to snap into it and get the place finished. There isn't so much outside work now. Bernd can help you a little every day."

"He's already said he would, Mrs. Almut. And Hans and Dieter and the Cellar Rats have been out a couple of times, so there's practically nothing but the stove left to do."

"Fine," Mrs. Almut said. "Now off to the kitchen with you. We women still have a lot to talk about."

"What about a residence permit?" Margret asked.

"My favorite sport is battling with officials; I'm world's lightweight champion at it. Besides which we have what is known in officialese as a 'privately fabricated dwelling.' And we need your mother badly. All of Hellborn and Dietholz will want her for sewing, and Rowan Farm most of all. But I have other plans besides. The pastor's wife and I have long thought we ought to set up a sewing school for the

refugee women. But we needed someone to conduct it. And
Joey can go to school in Hellborn for the next few years.
But what are we going to do about Andrea? She can go into town on the bus every day, but she'll have to wake up
awfully early. I know the driver; he'll stop for her. Still she
won't be able to ride back until five o'clock at night."

"That's no great difficulty," Margret said. "She can
surely stay at the Sauers until five. She has to help Lenchen
with her homework anyway."

"Well, you see, it's all going to work out. On the whole
it's a good thing the city is evicting your mother. Rowan
Farm will certainly profit by it, and so will you two, I
hope."

"Mrs. Almut," Margret said, "you're . . . you're really
the most wonderful . . ." Suddenly her face darkened. "Oh
dear, oh, it's terrible! I'd forgotten all about it. You see, we
have another child now."

"Another child! Good Heavens, where from?"

"Not a permanent child," Margret said dispiritedly. "But
I'm very much afraid he'll want to become a permanent one.
Hans Ulrich."

"Oh well, if that's all. One child more or less won't bother
us."

"But how are we going to feed them all?"

"They'll get ration cards here just as well as there. And
there'll always be a little extra for them here. Our cellar is
well stocked with potatoes and cabbage and winter vege-
tables, and you and Kathrin put up a whole barrel of sauer-
kraut. You already have a sheep and some day it will be giving milk. During the winter Matthias will have to build you
a small shed next to the sheepshed, so you can have a hen-

yard. There's nothing to stop you from keeping a few rab-bits, too, maybe angoras—the wool does very well when spun together with sheep wool. And maybe you'd feel like starting up our old bee house. During the war I gave up beekeeping because it was too much work for me, but Kathrin swears to this day that the bee witch lured away my swarms. And then your mother will certainly get extra food from her customers now and then. No, I wouldn't worry about that; they'll be better off here than in town."

"And suppose Father comes?" Margret said.

Mrs. Almut's face became grave. She had talked with Bernd about the card from Dr. Lechow, and Bernd had not been very hopeful. "The card is almost a year old," he had said. "I know what every month in camp can mean. And they're hardly likely to let a doctor go as long as he can stand on his feet."

"If your father comes," Mrs. Almut said, starting up her wheel again, "there's still room for him in the Ark, and he'll find work to do. Old Dr. Mengel in Dietholz has been dead for almost a year now, but although there are scads of young doctors, there don't seem to be any who want to take up practice in such an out-of-the-way place. Once a week a doctor comes out from town so people can consult him, but that's all we have."

"Father can do other work, too," Margret said. "He's handy at almost everything. He can do carpentry and elec-tric wiring and even repair radios. And he's a great gardener. He had the finest roses anywhere in our neighborhood, and some of his own hybrids, too, and he always raised medici-nal plants in Mother's kitchen garden. Mummy used to complain every year because there was hardly room enough for her tomatoes and beans and peas. I'm not worried about Father. If he can't find any practice, he'll do something else. Oh, if only he were back, Mrs. Almut."

At the Ark the boys set to work furiously. On the following Friday Matthias brought Dieter back with him from town, and they went together to Mariazell to fetch the potter and his firebrick. Then the three built the double stove. Bernd Almut came to inspect it and said the huge tile structure was so sturdy you could warm yourself just by looking at it.

In Margret's room the two lower bunk beds had to be taken out so that there would be room for the beds from Parsley Street, which Mrs. Lechow was bringing with her.

After talking things over with Mrs. Almut, Mrs. Hertrich and Mrs. Sauer, Mother had agreed to move out to Rowan Farm. Actually she was overjoyed and relieved not to have to move into the horrible barracks, and to have all her family together again. She had hesitated only because she feared she would be too much of a burden for Mrs. Almut. But these doubts were soon banished. Once Mrs. Almut had set her mind on anything, she could marshal irresistible arguments for it. The way she put the whole matter, it would seem that it was entirely for the advantage of Rowan Farm that Mrs. Lechow should move out there. "And after all," Mrs. Almut said as a final point, "two of the children are now as much mine as yours." All in all, Mother had allowed herself to be persuaded, and it seemed to Margret that she suddenly looked much younger.

And so one day Andrea and Joey and Hans Ulrich were told about the great news.

Andrea hopped from one foot to the other, and Joey bounced on the old sofa till it creaked and groaned.

"Are we taking everything?" Andrea asked.

"Can I sleep in the same room with Matthias, and Hans Ulrich too?" Joey asked. "Is it far to school, is there much school or will we have time to really do things?"

"And how am I going to get to school?" Andrea cried.

"Mrs. Sauer is willing to have you board with them," Mother said. But at that Andrea's face became so long, so terribly long, that Mother added quickly, "Or else you'll have to get up very early in the morning and go to the road in the dark and cold and wait there for the bus from Dietholz. You can ride back in the afternoon at five. Mrs. Sauer will give you lunch if you help Lenchen with her homework."

"Lunch for no ration stamps?" Andrea asked.

"Yes, for no ration stamps."

"Then I'll do it, I'll get up at six every morning, I don't care, but I won't stay alone in town. Hurray, hurray! We're moving into Noah's Ark. Didn't I always say Matthias should build an Ark for us!"

"And will we strew more pebbles behind us for Father?" Joey asked.

Hans Ulrich, who had been staying with the family for only a few days and still looked pale and spindly, asked again and again, "Are you really going to take me with you? You're not kidding me?"

"You'll stay with us till Christmas anyway," Mrs. Lechow said. "Then we'll see. And what red cheeks you'll get out there. Mountain air is the best thing for pale little boys. But you must promise me one thing, that when you go back to Mrs. Hertrich you'll be very, very fond of her."

"I think I can be a lot fonder of her if I'm with you," Hans Ulrich said sincerely, and for the first time there was a gleam of his old rascal's self in his brown eyes. "You mustn't forget that measles is a dangerous disease and it can come back if you don't get a long enough time to recover."

"All right, you three," Mrs. Lechow said, "sit down and I'll tell you how we're going to arrange everything."

And how wonderfully Mother could tell about it. The children listened with shining eyes. Mrs. Hertrich had promised to lend her a truck and Hans Ulrich's favorite truck driver to do the moving out to the farm. They would only take essentials, because so much of the furniture of the Ark was built in. They'd take the beds and linen, some chairs, dishware and pots.

"And all the books from the storeroom," Andrea said. "And those from the parlor too; the other people don't need them."

"Maybe not all, but some."

"And the sofa and the knickknacks from the parlor."

"Oh no," Mother said, "not those. Those must stay in the family. But we'll take the linen from the chests and cupboards and some of the clothes and curtains in mothballs . . ."

"Some? Why not all?"

"Mrs. Hertrich has given us so much that we don't need them. And with the rest," Mother said mysteriously, "we'll make ourselves a marvelous Christmas. You must talk to Mother Maria Magdalena, Andrea, and ask her to come here—she's in charge of refugee relief for the convent. Think of how happy those things will make so many people."

"Maybe there'll be something left for my foster mother?" Hans Ulrich asked.

"Certainly," Mrs. Lechow said. "Why shouldn't there be. But now go to sleep, children; I have a great deal to do."

CHAPTER FIFTEEN

Merry Christmas

ONCE MORE Margret was impatient. She ought to have learned this year that there was a time for everything, that things must grow and ripen. And she had learned it, but waiting was still hard for her. "If only Mother were here," she kept thinking. "If only Father would come home." Every day she looked out for the letter carrier. Every evening she stood by the stone bench and looked toward the East. And her young heart beat impatiently.

Often she bothered her brother. "Aren't you finished with the Ark yet? Can't we go and get Mother yet?"

Matthias answered, "We can't do miracles, old nag. We're still waiting for the stove top that Hans has to get for us."

Sometimes Margret overcame her shyness and spoke to young Bernd Almut when he came into the cowbarn while she was milking, or when he happened to be sitting alone in the kitchen weaving baskets of willow switches with his big, skillful hands. The willows were a reddish-brown, and he would finish off the top of the basket with a narrow edging of light-colored peeled twigs.

"What beautiful baskets you make," Margret said. "You make the border so pretty. Joseph and Matthias can't make them so well."

"I learned how in Russia."

"So that's where you learned it. How long did it take you to come here from Russia?"

"Very long. When we reached German soil, they put us into a hospital first thing. There many of us . . ."

"Died?" Margret asked softly.

Bernd nodded. They were both silent for a while. Then Margret asked, "Did you hear that the Hellingers' Franz came home yesterday. There are always some coming back alive. And a year ago Father was still living."

One morning Margret went to visit Marri in her house in the woods. Marri knew that Mother was coming, and she had heard about Father's postcard. "And how is Joey, the little fellow?" she asked. "He'll be comin' to see me, won't he?"

Margret asked, "Has the woodpecker knocked again as it did when Bernd came home? Or—has the owl hooted?"

"Wait," Marri said. "Waitin' is a bitter weed, but the fruit is sweet."

At last the day came. Dieter's boys had come from town and fixed the iron stove top in place on the kitchen stove, and heated it up for a test. In the kitchen there was even a small brick oven built into the chimney, so that really nothing stood in the way of the family's moving in.

Toward ten o'clock in the morning of the appointed day the Hertrichs' truck backed up to the gate at Rowan Farm, with the family and all their possessions aboard. Then the unpacking and arranging began, and each new member of the household was shown where to put his things. In the "women's room" two of the beds from Parsley Street were placed, one along the right wall and one along the left, and each bed had a bunk above as a second story. Mother would sleep in one of the beds and Margret and Andrea would alternate in the other. "But if the winter is as cold as last year we'll sleep together; it's easier to keep warm," Andrea said.

They had even brought with them a few bedside rugs, and a small carpet for the living room. The sofa was already installed there and gave a comfortable look to the room. The stove was lit and Caliph lay on the bench in front of it, while Ate and Bashka kept a respectful distance.

In the stern of the Ark, the men's quarters, a lively dispute was going on because of course each of the boys wanted to sleep on top. The third bed had been moved in there and Bernd and Matthias had taken out one of the lower bunks. Matthias had no objection to sleeping in a real bed with a mattress. As far as he was concerned, both the boys could have a top bunk, but Margret wanted to reserve one of the upper beds for visitors—since a lower bunk was so much easier to make.

"Let me have the upper one," Hans Ulrich pleaded.

"What do you mean, I want it," Joey shouted.

They might have started a good hand-to-hand fight over it. But Hans Ulrich was still so pale and skinny that a tussle would have been no fun. "I've just been sick and have to get better," he said pathetically. "And the higher up I am, the better for me. Mummy said mountain air would do me good."

"You can take turns," Margret decided. "One of you one week, the other next week. And let me tell you this, on Rowan Farm everybody has to lend a hand. You must make your own beds and keep your room spotlessly clean, like sailors on a ship, understand? And every Saturday you can sweep the yard; we've needed a couple of stable boys for that for a long time."

"Sure," Hans Ulrich said.

"Sure thing," Joey said. "And if the ponies need a little exercise, just mention the matter and we'll take them out for a ride."

Since there was nothing for the boys to do and they were only getting in the way, they ran off to say hello to the animals and to visit Marri, to whom Hans Ulrich had to be introduced. "Maybe she won't like you the way she does me," Joey said. "And then she might turn you into a pig. But don't worry, I'll have her change you back again."

Andrea went about singing and unpacking the boxes of books, since this seemed to her the most pressing task. The colorful bindings in the built-in bookcases gave the living room a wonderfully pleasant and homelike air.

Then she flitted off again to help with the rest of the unpacking. Moving in was great fun, she thought. She found her mother kneeling on the floor and taking dishware out of a box. "Look at this," Mother said, "we have all of Mrs. Verduz's painted stoneware, all the pretty peasant plates and cups and bowls. Her relatives didn't care for these things at all. They preferred to take the forget-me-not service from the parlor." The sturdy dishes looked charming on the shelves in the kitchen; they were just right for the Ark.

As soon as everything was unpacked and the Ark put in

order, Mother sat down at her sewing machine and began
working her way through the mountain of clothes in Mrs.
Almut's sewing basket. Out of every two old aprons she
made one new one. She freshened up Mrs. Almut's blue
dresses so that they looked neat and pretty again. Every remnant was made into collars. Shirts for Bernd were patched,
and bedsheets mended. Meanwhile the kettle boiled on the
stove and Caliph unashamedly lay in the middle of the
clothes basket and purred. Every few days Mrs. Almut came
and fetched a whole heap of freshly repaired and ironed
clothes, and she said again and again, "Didn't I tell you how
badly we've needed you here. But I'm watching you like
Cerberus. You have no idea how the demand for your serv-
ices is building up."

Before long the pastor's wife came around and asked
about the sewing class for the women of the neighborhood.
She would gladly turn over the parish meeting hall in Dietholz to such a class, and there was an urgent need for the
women of Dietholz to be taught how to convert old clothes
to new.

She and Mrs. Almut sat beside Mrs. Lechow's sewing
machine and admired her work. They were awed by her
competence and ingenuity. "We could never begin to do
these things," they said. They were neither of them any good
at sewing, they confessed, but every family had a pressing
clothes problem, and getting Mrs. Lechow to teach a class
was the only hope of solving it.

"In order to make attendance as convenient as possible,"
the pastor's wife said, "we'll suggest that the class meet once
a week in Dietholz and once at the Hellborn schoolhouse.
The schoolteacher's wife will help publicize the class, too."

The first Tuesday class could scarcely be called a success. Only five women turned up, and they sat around rather stiffly and on their guard while Mrs. Lechow demonstrated how to cut out children's jackets, slippers and knickerbockers from the materials they had brought along, and suggested embroidering the finished clothes with remnants of colored yarn. But on Friday at the Hellborn schoolhouse a few more women showed up, whether from curiosity or for practical reasons. And gradually something developed that nobody would have thought possible: the Catholic women of Hellborn and the Protestant women of Dietholz, the farm women and the refugee women, met in perfect harmony twice a week, and were so busy with their stitching and chatting that they forgot there were any dividing lines between them.

They sang Christmas carols together, and were surprised to find how many songs they had in common. "Well, well, whoever would have thought you used the same carols as us," a Hellborn woman said. And the pastor's wife smiled happily and said, "We also have the same Christ Child; just ask your pastor about that."

"So you're Joey's mother," the schoolmaster's wife said to Mrs. Lechow one day. Mother thought, now I'm going to hear a thing or two. But she bravely admitted her relationship, and said, "Yes, Joey's, and more or less Hans Ulrich's. Has your husband already decided to hand in his resignation?"

"Not exactly. He says if he had to manage a whole class of such boys he'd rather go out and break rocks. But among thirty others, he says, they do pretty well and have about the same effect as yeast in bread. They're not exactly the stars of

the class in the three R's, but they're full of life, he says, and
they ask questions and want to get to the bottom of everything. It's stimulating for these country children whose
minds are rather slow."

That evening, when Mother came home, the two boys
were sitting on the coffer bench by the stove, rather green
in the face and oddly quiet, carving with terrifyingly large
knives at some bits of wood. Probably a Christmas surprise,
Mother thought.

"What's the matter with you?" she asked with concern.
"Are the two of you ill?"

Andrea, who was sitting at the table doing a school theme,
said, "They were when I came home. Just smell them."

"For Heaven's sake, have they been playing in the manure
pile again?"

No, that was not it. Instead they had spent the afternoon
hours trying out the little pipe they had gotten in a swap
from Otto Smith who said he'd given up smoking after a
hard struggle. The fact was, it was all Joseph's fault. Why
did Joseph have to keep his home-raised tobacco in the haymow over the pony stable, and tobacco that wasn't even
properly cured yet?

It was at this point in the story that they lost Mother's
sympathy. "Smoking in the haymow!" she cried out. "Are
you mad? If Matthias hears about that he'll tan your hides
for you. I have a good mind to tell him."

"Andrea is a horrid old tattletale," Joey said.

But then they both pleaded so earnestly for Mother not to
tell Matthias, and swore such terrible oaths that they would
never never never do it again, that Mother softened and said
she thought they had already been punished. "As for you,

MERRY CHRISTMAS   235

Hans Ulrich, you're healthy as a young ox again. Before
Christmas I'm going to take you back to Mrs. Hertrich."

"But Mummy," Joey said concernedly, "how can you say
that when he's just been so sick?"

"Yes, I might catch measles all over again," Hans Ulrich
said. "And the second time you're like to die of it. And besides I want to be right here at home for Christmas."

"But you'll get lots more presents at the Hertrichs',"
Andrea pointed out.

"Don't need any," Hans Ulrich said.

Mother looked at him. "At home," he had said. At bottom
she had known for a long while that before Christmas she
would have to go to see Mrs. Hertrich about Hans Ulrich's
coming back. And she knew what the decision would be,
too. Poor Mrs. Hertrich with her loneliness and all her in-
stincts of a loving grandmother—Mrs. Lechow felt so sorry
for her. What a sacrifice and act of generosity Mrs. Hertrich
was going to make—to give up the child and yet go on pro-
viding for him. But after all, Mrs. Hertrich was much taken
up nowadays with making visits to Mrs. Krikoleit's children
and the Bennowitz' sick little girl, so that she was not so
alone as she used to be. Blessings had certainly come out of
that little suitcase. As for Mrs. Lechow herself, she could not
help seeing it as the work of Providence. She had had five
children and lost one, and now she would be having five
again.

That year the sisters' birthdays were celebrated on the
second Sunday of Advent, December 7, which came right
in the middle of the two birthdays. Five days before Margret
had found a slip of paper attached to the handle of her milk-

ing pail. It read, "Good for fifteen hatching eggs in March."
But there were more tangible presents. In spite of the pres-
sure of work Mother had found time to fix over for the girls
the two dresses she had received from Mrs. Hertrich, the
red one for Andrea and the lavender-blue one for Margret.
They were laid out in the living room on Sunday morning
when the children came in for breakfast. The Advent wreath
hung beneath the iron chandelier Matthias had found for
the Ark, and on the table stood a peasant jug filled with
pine branches, and a large cake that Kathrin had brought
over before anyone was up. There was also a jar of honey
that Marri had brought, so that everyone had a gala breakfast.

Margret looked at the lavender dress, brushed her hand
over its surface and held it up against her. At last she tried
it on and decided she didn't look bad at all in it. She would
wear it, she thought, for the dance to be held in Dietholz,
for which the Cellar Rats were already booked. That is, if
Mother let her go. But with Matthias and Bernd and Dieter
there, Mother would certainly let her. After all, she was fifteen years old now.

As always in this period before Christmas, there was a
great deal of social life. One week day Andrea came back
on the bus with Lenchen, Dieter and Tim. They were
greeted with loud shouts of joy and plied with the fragrant
blackberry tea which was always ready for Andrea, to thaw
her out when she came home. Margret cut bread and set out
honey, and Mother stopped sewing to come in and sit down
with the children. "How are you, Lenchen?" she asked.
"What are the Cellar Rats doing, Dieter? Have you written
any more songs, Tim? Can you stay overnight?"

"We're getting along, aren't we, Tim?" Dieter said. "They keep us pretty busy, with Christmas coming. We play at some office party almost every day, and that always means a good meal without ration stamps. We're playing twice a week for the Americans at their club now, and once a week at the German Youth Club they've started. We don't have much time or we would have come out long ago to bring our birthday present." He took a music notebook out of his pocket and laid it on the table in front of the girls. "A new Christmas song," he said. "Text by Tim, music by Dieter. It isn't hard to sing; let's try it out right away. But wait a minute, where are Matthias and Bernd?"

"They're having a calf," Joey said importantly.

"And day before yesterday they had a colt," Hans Ulrich said. "They were up half the night in the stable. It looks just like Lumpi—want to see it?"

Just then the door opened and Matthias and Bernd came in from the barn, both of them dirty and tired. But that did not stop them from getting their violins to try out the new song. Hulda had just had a fine heifer calf, they reported.

"Wonderful," Margret said happily; she considered that Hulda's having a heifer was a special favor to herself. "Then our stock will gradually be getting back to normal."

"You've already become a regular farm woman," Dieter said, "even though you don't look a bit like one."

Margret laughed and glanced at her rough, red hands. "Well, I wouldn't want to be anything else," she said.

Then they practiced the new song. It was easy to sing and play at sight, but they had to start over several times, for Dieter was unrelenting as always when it came to getting music right. Mother, too, joined in the song, and in a short

time the pure, clear notes of the new carol rang out from the
Ark.

> *Happily Thy mother smiles at Thee*
> *Though her cloak and shoes are ragged as can be.*
> *"Do not weep, do not weep, baby mine.*
> *House and home are far and the stall so drear,*
> *Thou'lt be warmed by ox and ass standing near,*
> *Softly wrapped in their breath, baby mine.*
> *Let the world judge harshly wrong and right,*
> *Bright in darkness shines Thy sweet mercy's light.*
> *Take this crust of bread humble worship brings,*
> *Bread of poverty. Hark, the angel sings:*
> *Crowns of Princes fade in Thy radiant shine,*
> *Son of man, child of God, baby mine."*

"And now," Dieter said, when they were through practicing the song, "how about trying out some dance steps?"

"But not here," Mother cried out in horror. "There isn't
room enough. See whether Mrs. Almut will let you use the
big hall."

They rushed over to the house and almost trampled down
Mrs. Almut, who was crossing the yard. "Can we practice
dancing in the hall?" they asked.

"Certainly, go ahead," she said. And in a moment they
had cleared away the hall furniture and were ready for
dancing. "It's a good idea for us to learn, too," Andrea com-
mented to Lenchen. "Maybe next year we can go out dancing with Margret and Matthias."

And then Dieter began playing, and when he played a
hippopotamus could have danced. Their feet became light
even in their heavy shoes, and their hearts carefree and gay.

Joey and Hans Ulrich sat on the stairs and called out criticisms of the dancing. They probably would have gone on all night if Kathrin had not returned from a visit to Hellborn and stood almost petrified at the door. "Dancing before Holy Week. Why, I'd think you'd be ashamed to show your faces. Six o'clock and not a cow milked yet or a pig fed, Margret!"

Still laughing and with hot cheeks, they all scattered— Margret in the lead with a milk pail on each arm.

From then on they practiced Christmas carols every night in the Ark. And on the last Sunday before Advent, after the evening milking, they made a second try at going carol-singing. Circumstances were a lot better than they'd been the Christmas before. As they started off through the woods, the new half moon shone down upon them. They had to walk fast, for they were planning many visits. First they went to the old priest of Mariazell, Father Mendel, whose house stood beside the church, high upon the hill. There they were invited to coffee. Then they called on the blacksmith and his young wife, who stuffed their pockets full of apples and cookies. And then they went on to their friend the shepherd, for whom they had to sing his favorite, *The First Noel,* twice. He wanted to keep them, but they had to be getting on. "We'll come to see you again right after Christmas," Margret said as they left. "I have a lot to ask you about, as usual. Belinda's going to lamb early in February this year. I only hope it won't be as hard a winter as last, or how will I ever raise those lambs?"

"Don't worry about it," the shepherd said. "What's meant to live lives, if people don't interfere too much."

In the rectory at Dietholz the five blond, cleanly washed

children of the pastor stood in a row like organ pipes and
listened with shining eyes to the carol-singing. They were
overjoyed when Margret invited them to join in when there
were songs they knew. They too wanted to keep the carolers
all night. At the end each brought out a little present: a tin-
sel star, a cotton lamb, an apple, a handful of nuts and a
brown honey cake. "Are you coming back tomorrow?" the
youngest called out as they tramped off down the snow-
covered village street.

Then they went to Marri's. Singing, they stood under the
snowy trees which cast blue shadows in the moonlight. The
door opened. Lamplight fell upon the snow, as though someone had poured out a pail of golden honey. Marri stood in
the doorway, so amazed and pleased she could not say a
word. Softly the song died away among the trees:

> *Take this crust of bread humble worship brings,*
> *Bread of poverty. Hark, the angel sings:*
> *Crowns of Princes fade in Thy radiant shine,*
> *Son of man, child of God, baby mine.*

Finally they went back to Rowan Farm and sang there as
they had sung last year. And this time, too, Mrs. Almut
would not let them stand out in the cold. They all had to
gather in the hall, and it seemed strange indeed to Margret
that it was already a full year since she had first sung here.
It was all the same as it had been last year: the professor
opened his door and listened, Kathrin and Joseph came in
their stocking feet and sat down on the lowest step of the
stairs. But now Mother sat with Mrs. Almut in her room,
and Bernd was here—when last year no one had known
whether Bernd would ever come home again.

Once more they sang all their favorite songs, and at the end Dieter's and Tim's own carol.

"And now let's celebrate the anniversary of our first meeting!" Mrs. Almut said, and they all trooped into her room for hot tea with rum—even the two little boys were given a few sips—and a huge plate full of honey cakes, and they spent a long happy evening together while the candles flickered above green pine branches which filled the whole room with their fragrance.

Two days till Christmas Eve. And school was already out for the holidays, and there was plenty of snow for sliding. But only Hans Ulrich and Joey had time to play around outside—for they had been good boys and already done their Christmas week homework. In the house people were scouring and polishing and baking, and in the Ark people were scouring and polishing and sewing. Margret had so much work she was almost out of her mind, for the new calf turned out to be terribly backward about learning to drink from the pail. But it was always like this before Christmas—with everybody having too much to do and nobody knowing how he was ever going to manage to get everything done. If it were not like that, it would not have been a real Christmas. Everybody seemed to be preparing all sorts of surprises, although this Christmas, the third postwar Christmas, it was still not possible to buy anything in the way of presents. Sooner than worry everybody with having to get too many presents, it had been agreed to provide a single present for each. Each name would be written down on a folded piece of paper. The pieces of paper were placed in Mrs. Almut's old fur hat, and everyone drew a slip with the name of the person for whom he was to prepare a present. Then there were the Cellar Rats to be thought about, too.

There was a great deal of whispering and giggling and mystification, a great deal of crackling paper and whittling of wood and snipping of cloth, and through it all came the fragrance of things baking in the kitchen, and the sound of Joey and Hans Ulrich singing, humming or whistling incessantly, "Christmas is coming, Christmas is coming, tomorrow will be the day!"

"It isn't tomorrow at all," the sisters would complain all day long. "Stop that awful noise, it's driving us mad."

"All right, if you feel that way about it," the boys retorted. "Then we'll go to the barn; at least the calf appreciates music."

"You leave my calf alone, you pests," Margret called after them, and they called back, "All right, then we'll go sliding again. Our pants are soaking wet anyway."

Offended, they went out into the soft white wintry world. Black crows sat on the posts around the pasture, peered at them with tilted heads and then flew off at the last minute, cawing hideously. It seemed they wanted no more to do with two little boys than those nasty womenfolk in the house.

Sliding on the seat of their pants and throwing snowballs at one another was good sport, but they would much rather have had skis. In fact, if only they had skis it wouldn't have been necessary for them to appear at the kitchen door every half hour and modestly ask whether there weren't any burnt cookies to be had. "We don't mind eating the burnt ones," they said with a pleading look at the bakers.

There were still two whole days to Christmas Eve—how were they ever going to stand it. They were almost inclined to wish there were school for those two days. Think of reaching such a low point! Still, school would have kept time from creeping along the way it was doing.

They slid down the slope, they ran to the stone bench a hundred times and looked for the letter carrier, because Margret had said there would just have to be another card from Father as a Christmas present for Mother, and the boys were eager to be the bearers of this Christmas present. It was the twenty-second already, so if a card were to come at all, it was about time. But there was no sign of the letter carrier. Or was there?

Of course, there he was, coming up the highway, walking slowly, his back bent. The boys ran to meet him. But then they realized it was not the letter carrier; it was a total stranger. Disappointed, they were about to turn back. Then they saw that the man was waving and calling to them. They stood still. He came closer.

"Hello," the man said.

"Hello," the boys said.

He looked like a tramp. His shoes were held together with string. He was limping slightly, as though he had a sore foot. On his head he wore a mangy fur cap, and in his hand he carried a stout stick.

"Do you know the way to Rowan Farm?" the man asked.

"We can show you," Joey said. "You see, we happen to live there."

"So you happen to live there. Then do you happen to know a family by the name of Lechow?"

"My name is Lechow," Joey said, pounding his chest with his fist. "Joey Lechow."

"So I thought!" the man said. "And how is your mother?"

"She's well. We were hoping so much for a card from Father for her, for Christmas. You see, he's in Russia."

"Why, haven't you had many cards from him?"

"Oh no. Just one. And that one's a year old."

"You have brothers and sisters, don't you, Joey?"

Joey counted on his fingers. "Matthias, he's the nursery apprentice here, and Margret is the kennel maid, and Andrea, only she's nothing yet."

"No others?"

"No— Yes, we used to have Christian, but I don't remember about him any more."

"And now they have me," Hans Ulrich said. "Only we don't have a father yet."

They were already passing through the gate to the yard. The boys ran across to the barn; the man remained standing alone in the snow. But a moment later he saw a tall girl come out of the barn. She placed her pails down in the snow and approached him.

"Whom do you wish . . ." she began. And then she stopped. She stared at him, and her face turned red. "Father!" she said. Then she took hold of his hand and pulled him along behind her. "Come to Mummy, quick."

Mother was sitting at her sewing machine. Margret opened the door and thrust the man in. He took off his fur cap and laid it on the bench beside the stove. Then he went up to the sewing machine. Mrs. Lechow's hands dropped to her lap. A pair of scissors fell to the floor with a clatter. She sat still, staring at the man, her eyes growing bigger and bigger. It seemed as if the person who had come in were not a ragged, dirty vagabond, but the most glorious of the angels who gather around the throne of God. Softly, Margret closed the door behind her. Then she went to the barn to tell Matthias. . . .

There was a glorious, happy Christmas Eve feast in Noah's Ark and on all of Rowan Farm. Nobody asked that day what cares the future might bring. And what presents there were for a celebration that would have been unbelievably happy even without any presents at all. There were handsome checked shirts made of old bedspreads, warm slippers made of old window drapes, wooden clogs to wear in the barn, mittens and heavy woolen socks. There was a fine knitted cap for Mrs. Almut, so that she could dispense with her disgraceful old stocking, and a handwritten book of poems for Bernd, and for Matthias a real tobacco pipe— after all, a man had to have one. Tucked into its box was a note on which was printed: "From Joey and Hans Ulrich, because we have quit smoking."

The silver moon stood high in the sky when, late Christmas Eve, Margret once more made the round of all her animals to wish each and every one a happy Christmas. She brought each one a treat, according to its taste. And afterward, as she did every day, she walked with Ate and Bashka to the stone bench and looked up at the stars, which tonight flickered rather dimly because the moon was so bright.

When she returned and closed the gate for the night, a long shadow darted across the yard. She climbed the steps to the Ark. Everyone was already asleep there, and all the lights were out. On the topmost step she made out a dark something in the shadow cast by the wall. She bent and picked it up. It was a basket, a beautifully delicate basket with a handle and a skillfully-worked white border, the kind of border that few people knew how to make. A basket for gathering berries and herbs and mushrooms. Margret held it up to the moonlight and looked at it, and it seemed to her that in spite of all the Christmas gifts she had still been wanting something, and that this basket answered the need. A slip of paper hung from the handle of the basket, and the moonlight was bright enough for her to read the handsome lettering which said:

MERRY CHRISTMAS TO MARGRET!

ML